CHRISTMAS MIRACLES

JOSEPH S. BONSALL

Copyright ©2012
Richards & Southern, Inc. and Joseph S. Bonsall

All rights reserved. No part of this book may be reproduced in any form or by any electronic or mechanical means, including information storage and the retrieval systems, without permission in writing from the publisher, except by a review who may quote brief passages in a review.

Reproduction of this book in whole or in part without the expressed written permission of Richards & Southern, Inc. and Joseph S. Bonsall is strictly forbidden.

Library of Congress Control Number: 2012949850

ISBN 978-0-9856601-4-7 (Paperback)
ISBN 978-0-9856601-3-0 (Electronic Book)

Published by: Richards & Southern, Inc.
P.O. Box 37 Goodlettsville, TN 37070

Executive Producer - *Terry Calonge*
Project Coordinator - *Jeremy DeLoach*
Project Design - *Dennis Davenport*

PRINTED IN THE UNITED STATES OF AMERICA

Table of Contents

Author's Note ....Page One

Eric and Emily..Page Five

Big Grin..Page Twenty Three

Little Jerry's Christmas...Page Forty Three

Private Bluegrass: A Christmas Story................................Page Fifty Five

Snowball.......A Christmas Miracle................................Page Seventy Nine

Little Jerry's Christmas ~ The Play..............................Page Ninety Seven

The Bell........A Christmas Commentary..........Page One Hundred Thirteen

The Carpenter's Choice ....An Epilogue......Page One Hundred Nineteen

Dedicated to:

The Eric and Emily's, Tolefson's, Little Jerry's, Billy Mellon's, and Marissa Errington's of this world . . .

May they find their miracles!

Author's Note

First of all, thanks to Terry Calonge and Richards and Southern for publishing this little book of short stories and miracles. Thanks to my business associate, dear friend, and book agent Kathy Harris for perusing the matter.

Thanks also to my wife, Mary Ann, my daughters, Sabrina and Jen, and my grandchildren, Breanne and Luke for their constant love and faith. And thanks to my singing partners Duane Allen, William Lee Golden, and Richard Sterban for their constant belief in and support of my writing. Thanks to friends like Darrick Kinslow for staying on me to "keep on writing!" Thanks as well to my dear parents, Joe and Lillie, for making every Christmas morning of childhood magical and precious for my sister Nancy and me, even though they did not have a lot of means at their disposal.

The spirit of Christmas and the spiritual meaning of the season have always meant the world to me. From the time I was little, every aspect of Christmas seemed to affect my life in a positive way. From the birth of Jesus Christ to Santa Claus and his magical sleigh, the little boy who dwells inside of me has been kept alive. I have always believed all things are possible, especially at Christmastime. The simple and miraculous birth of a child to a virgin in a stable opened the door to personal salvation and eternal life for everyone.

For me, the spirit of giving and celebration and good tidings of cheer has never faded. Not even a little bit. I believe in the good nature of people, and I honestly believe if more folks would allow that little girl or little boy within to come alive, and have just a little more of that childlike faith that Jesus spoke of, then there would be more miracles and the world would be a better place.

I guess that is why I love Christmas stories. The canvas with which to write upon is really quite alluring. That may be why some of my most successful writing seems to take place around Christmas. For more than twenty years The Oak Ridge Boys have engineered a mighty Christmas tour across this great country. Children of all ages come out to listen to songs about Santa, presents, cookies, and the birth of Jesus. I try to write a Christmas story or pertinent memoir every year during this time away from home, and this little book contains a few of them.

Thanks for reading. Merry Christmas and God bless!
Keep the child inside of you alive and well! (JSB)

Eric and Emily

Eric and Emily met by accident . . . literally. Eric had served America, as part of the fabled 82nd Airborne, for years and had just completed his last tour of duty in Afghanistan. He had served on bomb squads, recon patrols, and Special Ops and was even trained as a sniper, and not once was he ever wounded. In fact, Eric had never experienced one scratch on his body, until he came home from a tough war and was run over while jogging by Emily Sullivan.

Emily's little electric "baby car," as he called it, felt more like a troop carrier when it skidded out of control and sideswiped the young soldier, sending him flailing right into a ditch like a ragdoll. He actually thought for a moment that he'd stepped on an IED . . . but in North Carolina?

Emily was a civilian business administrator on base and was running late one morning when she took a curve a little too fast and sent the young (*and very handsome*) soldier flying.

"Thank God I didn't kill him," she thought, as she jumped out of her car and noticed right off that her victim, although bleeding from a gash in his head, was sitting up and, thankfully, breathing.

Eric was fully prepared to jump all over this guy when he suddenly looked up and beheld the face of the woman who would share the rest of his life.

"I am so sorry! Are you okay? I mean . . . I was just trying to . . . I mean it was stupid to be driving so fast, but I was running late, and . . . OH, MY GOD are you a soldier? I could have killed you . . . I might have . . ." Emily blurted. "Why are you smiling?"

All Eric could do was smile. This woman was just too cute and, although his head felt as if he had just taken a bullet in it, soon-to-be-retired First Lieutenant Eric Mason, a farmer's son from Emmet, Iowa, was most certain that he was already in love with this seemingly crazy woman. He stood up to introduce himself and fainted dead away.

Emily Sullivan became Mrs. Eric Mason just six weeks later.

An Iowa sunset seems as mysterious as it is beautiful. Every one seems to spin its own little story, and Emily had grown to love them. Sinking low above her husband's cornfields the waning sun seemed to reach out with one last effort and proceed to paint the western sky in a myriad of orange and yellow that stretched out as far as one could see. Each cloud became a little Monet or a Picasso type masterpiece.

The setting sun also indicated that Eric's work was through for the day. That sound of the big John Deere tractor shutting down was something she looked forward to every evening. Soon they would sit together on the back porch and quietly hold each other as the last rays of the day vanished into darkness. It was a precious time. It was a holy time.

Not that it has been an easy road for Emily to go from being Miss 'totally on her own' and relatively happy about it, to being an ex-grunt farmer's wife. Her adjustments were a big major deal.

First off, she was raised in Chicago by a single mom whose romance is written about in the encyclopedia under the heading "BUST!" To be honest, her mom did not like men at all and constantly preached to a young Em about the validity of staying far away from them and hoofing it on her own.

"Men are nothing but heartbreak," she would always say. "They are liars and completely self centered. WHAT WAS God thinking when he made them first!" Or, "Better to be alone than have to wait on an ingrate!" Or, "They are all cheaters . . . let your guard down and boom . . . heartbreak!"

Although her mom's rants brought a smile now, there was no doubt her influence on Emily was immense. After Emily graduated from Northwestern with a Masters in Business, her mom passed away following a long, hard battle with ovarian cancer. So Em decided to move far away to North Carolina, where she took a fabulous job at Fort Bragg Army Base, which was the home of the 82nd Airborne and U.S. Army Special Operation Headquarters, far from Chicago and all of the excess baggage that went with it!

Emily had a nice apartment over a beauty shop and drove a sensible Prius. She was putting all her faith in God for direction from here and figured He was certainly involved in the plan to sideswipe and wound a soldier. If not, she would have probably killed him. Anyhow, the event was life changing for her, and even now it was hard to believe.

Eric knew from "day one" that this woman was a different piece of work for sure. But, just like a soldier, he fell right on over the cliff for her. It was not just that she was beautiful, but there was a light that seemed to shine from her. He had known a few pretty sharp girls in Iowa, one in particular in Ames during the year he attended Iowa State. He really thought the world of Linda. But after he told her he was leaving school because his father was a much better Ag teacher than any professor—and besides he had a deep yearning to serve his country and planned on joining the Army—just like that she was off with a second string Cyclone quarterback.

It was probably for the best, because Eric had stuff to do before even thinking about settling down, much to the dismay of the insurgent Taliban in theater. Eric Mason was one tough strong farm boy and many paid with their lives for being anywhere in the area of any mission of which he was a part. He was good at it. He was the kind of man who was needed in this world of cruel and unusual enemies. He was a man who loved his God and loved his country.

So the transition for him was not a smooth one either. Eric was a trained Special Ops soldier with a one-track mind, and he had to learn fast that "my way or the highway" did NOT work very well with Emily Sullivan. But they persevered by adhering to a few very strict 'Emily rules.'

"We may butt heads, but our love comes first."

"Never hurt each other by saying things we don't mean."

And most importantly, "NEVER go to bed angry!" They never did!

They were overall about as close as a couple could be. It actually hurt to be more than a few yards apart. Always touching, always kissing, always listening to one another. When he looked deep into her eyes, he swore he could see her soul reflecting back at him, and she felt exactly the same.

Even their lovemaking was strong and giving. Nothing they did was ever embarrassing to one another, and the secret doors of both their minds and hearts were never closed. Quite to the contrary, every moment shared was wide open without even a hint of inhibition or apprehension.

This was true love on every level. The stuff of dreams. This was love that all of humanity longed for . . . hoped for . . . searched for . . . prayed for. Two human beings who walked together as one. One with God . . . one with creation . . . one with each other.

Then tragedy struck the Mason family. Within a few days of losing his mom, Eric also lost his dad. They had both been old and infirm, and it was right after his discharge that he went home to Iowa to bury them and to take over the family farm and implement business.

Emily was happy to go with him.

Eric worked the farm and handled the business. It was as if he were born for the job. And, in reality . . . he was. His parents had been great people, and he had learned so much from them. His mother had taught him how to love and how to appreciate God and His many blessings. His dad had taught him how to respect and love the land that God had provided. They were people of deep, abiding faith, who possessed a true Middle-American values' system that had been deeply imbedded inside of Eric.

He would NEVER let them down! Emily loved Iowa. She loved the people and she loved the land. She thought she might get a job at the university but, for now, she relished being a farmer's wife and thoughts of little Mason children running around the place started to occupy more and more of her thoughts and eventually her prayers.

We can never really make plans though can we? Every passing day brings a chance that everything we thought was certain and settled can change in a heartbeat. September 11, 2001 did that to the entire country. Not one thing in the paper that morning seemed relevant on the morning of the twelfth.

Stuff happens . . . events turn on a dime.

So it was on the day that Emily came home from the doctor to tell Eric the good news. That he was to become a father in about seven months.

Then the phone call came from the State Department.

"It's going to be a boy or a girl . . . I don't know yet . . . and what do mean you have to go on a mission? A MISSION? WHAT?" Emily blurted, tears streaming down her cheeks.

"Oh, honey, I am so happy." Eric was crying as well, as he pulled her closer to him. "This is a time to celebrate and to thank God for the miracle of birth and family. All life begins with Him, and I promise you I will be the best father a child can have."

She pushed him back a little. "You mean if you are HERE.

Why didn't you just say 'no.'" Emily sat down hard on the chair with her face buried in her hands. "We have a wonderful life, and now I could lose you."

"I promise that will not happen, Em. I will get this job done and come home as always. I believe somehow that this is part of God's will. We just need to trust Him, Em . . . as we have always done. Jess and Bonnie will help around here while I am gone. I just couldn't say no. I just couldn't." His voice began to sound distant at this point, but Eric knew he HAD to do this thing.

Jess and Bonnie Whitaker lived just over the rise and were the best friends the Mason family had. Eric knew he could count on them while he was back in Operations. The conference call that came had been from a higher-up at state, a general, and a commander at Bragg. They shared secrets with Eric that only nine other men like himself were privy to. It was at once exciting and scary, and Eric knew he had to say 'yes.' They gave him a choice but yet it somehow did not seem like a choice.

Anyhow . . . he was in!

They wanted ten highly trained ex-military commandos for a very special mission in Syria, of all places. They were to be inserted in-country with the help of the Israeli Mossad, and their mission would be to take out all the top leaders in the rogue Syrian Government, including the Prime Minister and the warlord President, who had already killed tens of thousands of his own people.

They would deploy in September and, hopefully, be home by Christmas. Every detail of the mission would be laid out for him when he arrived at Fort Bragg and, if he were to be caught, the United States would disavow any knowledge of his existence.

He told Emily none of this, of course.

* * *

Come early November, a very lonely and pregnant Emily Mason watched the Iowa sunset from her back porch. Bonnie Whitaker came over every day and helped her around the house and with the cooking. Bonnie's presence and always-positive spirit was much appreciated. She was "good people," as Emily's mom would have said, and so was Bonnie's husband.

Jess and his men had taken in all of Eric's corn and soybean crops and looked after the several hundred head of beef cattle on the three hundred acre Mason spread, while the Whitaker sons took care of the small store, at least part time. The little store called simply "Mason's" was closed much of the time right now, but it would hopefully pop back under Eric's care and expertise.

Emily felt a little kick or two as she stared at the fading daylight. Like most nights, she would sit here alone in the cool autumn air, long after dark descended upon the farm, and think of and pray for her husband. It was so hard for her. She missed him terribly and not even being able to hear his voice was simply maddening.

Emily was not a stupid woman. She knew he was somewhere dangerous and doing something extraordinary. Why? Because he could, and would. Because he loved his God and his country, even a bit more then he loved her and their unborn child.

Perhaps this should have hardened her heart a bit, but the residual aspect of that truth made her love and respect him even more. She was married to a very special man and she thanked God for him.

"Where are you, my husband? Are you safe? I miss you so much. Oh, Precious Jesus, hold him in your protective and everlasting arms right now. Guide him, look after him . . . he does love you, Lord. And he feels like he is doing your will. Lead him with your light, Heavenly Father, and bring him home to me. Please, Lord . . . please. Send an angel to watch over him." Emily prayed like this for hours almost every night until sleep overtook her.

From September 1st through October 12th, the training was

almost unbearable. It was like basic training all over again because they wanted to make sure this team was in shape. There were classroom meetings, tactical maneuvering, and weapons and explosives work from morning until night.

This bunch was turning into a well-honed unit that was capable of just about anything. To the casual observer they seemed like a bunch of SEALs or Rangers, or Airborne Special Ops guys doing routine stuff. But, beneath that façade, something very special was being honed and perfected.

The world community, including Russia and Iran, had no idea what to do about the mess in Syria. The United Nations was, as usual, applying band-aids that didn't stick, and every day more people were being slaughtered. The U.S. could not send in bombers or fighters or ground troops and there weren't enough Drones to solve this problem. So they utilized the old theory that a small, secret force of highly trained men with the right weapons and planning could get the job done. Just like SEAL Team Six did in taking out Bin-Laden. Except this time . . . nobody would realize who did what and to whom.

They called themselves the NightOwls. Silent and strong and deadly. Eric had to put Emily and his child and his farm totally out of his mind if he were to succeed. That was not easy.

"Lord, comfort them and, if it be Thy will that I can return to Iowa, I will be eternally grateful. I will serve you until the day I die . . . I promise!"

The NightOwls, accompanied by six Israeli secret service men, entered Syria through Turkey on November 28th.

* * *

Emily had decorated the house big time. She had a huge tree, and strings of lights dangled down and around from every nook and cranny. When she flipped the switch, their little farmhouse seemed like Disneyland. She was adding yet another ton of tinsel to the tree when, just like that, her water broke and it was time!

She called the Whitakers. On December 20th, around 8 p.m., young Samuel Sullivan Mason was born in the Estherville, Iowa hospital where his father had been born. And his father's father before him.

At that same time Sam's daddy was in it up to his ears and then some . . .

Everything went well from insertion to final mission. Never was a military operation pulled off so smoothly and with such expertise from the men involved. If all went well in the next few hours, the Israeli Mossad would be able to extract the NightOwls and this thing would be over.

They moved on the compounds under cover of darkness. They were split into two incredibly armed teams of five

NightOwls each. Over the next hour, there were explosions and gunfire and running and yelling. Death was everywhere.

Eric entered a well-lit room. He knew every corner. He even knew who would be there, and how many. He wasn't very far off either.

He took out seven men, utilizing heavy automatic rifle fire, and then drew his Glock 27 sidearm and immediately placed two rounds into the head of the Syrian President.

Eric was out of the room before the evil leader ever hit the ground. He was running into the courtyard when the explosion happened. He felt disoriented. Men were grabbing his arms and leading him somewhere. He reached for his sidearm, and it was gone . . . Things seemed slow and hazy, and all he could think about was Emily. He could see her face. Her eyes. He was touching her, kissing her . . .

When the haze cleared, he was sitting oddly alone in the grass somewhere. A man stood by him. A very tall man. Eric tried to speak, but nothing came out. The tall man was unarmed and stared at Eric.

Was that a robe? Have I been taken prisoner? Have I . . . ?

The soldier's mind was racing as he tried to process everything. He wanted to get up but could not.

All of a sudden this man began to speak. His voice was soft and yet it possessed a strange resonance. It seemed to echo a bit.

"I will quote His Holy Word unto you, Eric Mason. It says in Deuteronomy 33:27, the Eternal God is your refuge and underneath are the everlasting arms . . . it goes on to say that He will drive out your enemy before you, saying 'destroy him.' This you have done in good faith and in His Holy will. God has always needed men with a sword, and you have answered a clarion call. You did not have to do that . . . but you did."

"Is this a dream, sir," Eric asked, his voice seeming to return. "Am I dead? Are you an angel?"

"You are part right, Eric Mason, for I am a warrior such as you. To the best of my knowledge I have always been. I am to this day battling evil and darkness. I once fought a Prince of Persia for twenty-one days right on this very spot where you ended another demon's miserable life. I, sir, am the answer to your wife's prayers. Now go home, warrior, for unto you this day a son is born."

The man smiled and the light around him grew so bright that Eric had to shield his eyes.

"I am Michael, the archangel, sent to watch over you! Serve the Master!"

Then with a flutter of wings, he was gone.

Eric woke up on a cot in Tel Aviv, deep within Mossad headquarters.

"Thank God you are awake," whispered a fellow NightOwl.

"We are safe now, and the mission is accomplished. We ship home mañana!"

"What happened?" Eric asked

"Well, Corn Boy, you seemingly took a direct hit from a rocket propelled grenade. I ran to you expecting to find your body parts scattered all about and there you were, man . . . lying in the grass . . . breathing hard but not a scratch on ya!" said the NightOwl known only as Cricket.

"Casualties?" Eric was afraid to ask.

"We lost three men and three more shot up pretty bad. A few more scrapes and bruises here and there, except for you. Untouched brother! How did you manage that? You were more in the thick of it than most of us and really . . . you should NOT be here, bro!"

All Eric could do was smile.

Emily was watching her favorite news commentary show, *The Five on FOX,* when they broke in with the special report.

"Hello, everyone. This is Brit Hume. Last night a secret attack was carried out on the ruling government of Syria and killing . . ." Emily couldn't breathe.

"It a new day for Syria, as rebel troops have marched into Damascus celebrating the . . ."

"Oh, Sweet Jesus," she thought.

"Was it the Israeli's or was is, as some think, a United

States covert operation where a small force of . . ."

Emily fainted.

As her head cleared she thought she heard a distant voice speaking to her from deep inside her being.

"Answered prayers, woman . . . Serve the Master. For unto you is born . . ."

The voice trailed away, and Emily rose up only as far as her knees and prayed for hours.

Bonnie Whitaker came by to visit on Christmas morning. She brought pies and cakes and turkey and all kinds of goodies. Baby Sam seemed very happy to be a part of this magical morning and laughed at just about everything.

"Where is Jess this morning?" Emily asked.

"He will be here shortly. He has a special present for you!"

When Jess's Ford F-150 truck pulled up in the driveway Emily knew in her heart what that present would be.

"Answered prayers woman."

She flew out the door and into the cold Iowa December air. She was in his arms before he ever got completely out of the truck!

It was a blessed Christmas at the Mason farm in Emmet, Iowa that year. There was much prayer and thanksgiving. Eric was home and would never again leave this town.

Emily was ready to raise a family, starting with little

Samuel. Eric rocked him back and forth and wept as he pondered all that he had been through.

"It was Michael, the Archangel, Emily. It WAS him. He spoke to me. He quoted scripture, he spoke of you and he . . . he . . ."

"I know, honey, he spoke to me too. We are blessed beyond measure," Emily said, as tears of joy flowed once again.

"Serve the Master, he said. And I will, Em, until the day I die."

"We both will live in His light, and we will raise up Sam in the way he should go."

"Something tells me that boy is going to be very special." Eric smiled.

"Like his daddy . . . a miracle . . . without a scratch on him."

They laughed and kissed like teenagers as the lights blinked all around them, and the full moon and a new bright star appeared in the Eastern part of the massive Iowa sky.

Big Grin

James "Big Grin" Tolefson had once been a Naval Destroyer Commander. In this modern age of warfare he might have been referred to as a boat driver, however the title commander seemed to fit Grin like a custom suit. This man was INDEED a Commander in every sense of the word and in his day he not only commanded a U.S. Navy warship, but he also commanded the respect of all who served with him.

His men and his boat had been individually responsible for sinking three Japanese destroyers and one aircraft carrier, which might have helped to turn the tide in the battle of Okinawa during the bloody war for the Pacific during World War II. Yes, the Marines did their job on the land in places like Iwo Jima and Guadalcanal, but much of this war had been fought upon and under the seas. And Commander Tolefson was right there in the thick of the battle. In fact, his reconnaissance patrols during the battle for the Aleutian Islands in the treacherous Bering Sea early on were the stuff of legend.

Many thought he was the best, and he probably was. The seamen under his command gave him his nickname, because the guy just always seemed to be smiling. ALWAYS!

But Commander Tolefson was not smiling on this particular afternoon. The man the sailors referred to as Big Grin could not seem to find his way clear enough to navigate his vessel around a Luby's Cafeteria.

This was not the first time for such a mental lapse. Recently Jim had found himself lost and alone in the small park that was right across from his home. He had lived in that house by that park since 1952. He took an early morning stroll as he had done so many times before. He sat down to rest a on a park bench for a moment and closed his eyes. He let his mind drift around a bit and when he awoke, just a few minutes later, he did not know where he was. The man who had been so steady and sure and in command in his younger days now panicked and began to be afraid. A young fellow who knew the Tolefson family eventually came by and gently took him by the arm and led him back home to Grace.

On this day at Luby's, he had scooped up a fair amount of scalloped potatoes and corn into his plate and begun to walk back to his seat where Grace was seated with their neighbor friends, Renee and Carter Lewis. The four of them ate at Luby's together every other Saturday afternoon. Old Carter was a flyboy. He had flown B-24 bombers over Italy, and he and Jim had become good friends over the years despite the constant needling that one might expect between the two old veterans.

The constant bickering and chiding really got on the girls' nerves, but it was all in fun. They knew that both men had once lived in hell for a period of their young lives, so they let them blow off a bit of steam from time to time. Gracie and Renee knew these men would die for each other in a heartbeat. That is the kind of men they were. For better or worse, these two wonderful old women would look after their guys until death came between them. That was the kind of girls THEY were! Jim and Carter were the heart and soul of the Greatest Generation. They were elderly now, but once they had saved the free world, and they never gave up on each other . . . NEVER!

"Grace, why is Jim wandering around way over there with his plate of food?" asked Renee.

"Oh no." Grace thought. *"Not again!"*

"Must have lost his compass," said Carter. "I'll go and get him."

Despite his best efforts, Jim began to panic. He was lost again and had no idea which way to turn. He heard Carter call out to him and proceeded to drop his plate of food, scattering corn and potatoes all over the floor. He began to cry. A man who only wept in his dreams was now weeping like a child in a public restaurant. It seemed like everyone in the whole darn place was staring right at him.

"Rough seas, sailor?" asked Carter, as he placed his arm around the shoulder of his friend.

"Take me home, man . . . take me home now."

On their way to the car, Grace Tolefson pulled her rarely used cell phone out of her handbag. Julie had given it to her as a birthday gift to use in case of an emergency. Grace autodialed her daughter's phone number as Carter helped her husband into the passenger seat of their old, but very dependable, Chevy Impala.

Julie Tolefson Stinson was a veterinarian with a very successful practice. She was married to a firefighter and had given her mom and dad two wonderful grandsons who were both big boys now. Her life was busy, to say the least, but being a senior partner at the animal hospital allowed her to rely on several younger vets to handle the major workload, therefore giving her more time to herself and to her husband Randy, who although tough as nails and built like a brick abutment, was also a very needy soul and required her special attention. Especially after a big fire or when lives were lost.

Most firefighters put in their twenty years and retired, but Randy Stinson had already put in thirty, and Julie figured that, although he was now well into his fifties, Randy just might be a "hose carrier" for life. But, raising two kids, supporting a husband, and taking care of a business were a piece of cake compared to the constant strain and heartbreak of seeing her loving father begin to loose his mind. She pulled her Toyota into the driveway of the home of her childhood and parked right behind her parents' Chevrolet, just as they were all getting out of the car.

She ran to her father who seemed just fine.

"Hi, Peaches, why in the world are you sill driving that Japanese piece of crap? If I were still in command I would drop a charge right on top of that thing and sink it down into the briny deep. ARRRGGGH! Yes, I would."

"Oh, Daddy, I love you so much," she said as she threw her arms around his neck. Ever since she was a little girl he had talked like a pirate to her, and she always loved it. "Are you okay, Dad?"

"Aye, girl, I YAM! Just took a blow to me starboard side, but I'll be rum runnin' again by dawn."

He looked deep into the eyes of his only child and went on. "Yeah, I am okay, honey. I think. I mean I feel just fine right now, but I was lost at sea for a few minutes there. It's getting kind of scary."

Julie's eyes began to tear up. This hurt so bad. One hears of Alzheimer's all of the time but doesn't think much about it until the horrible disease hits their own family broadside. There is a price for everybody to pay. Not just the one who is fading away.

"Well, let's get off the street and into the house," implored Grace.

The Lewises sadly walked on home, while Grace and her daughter helped the "Old Salt" get into bed.

* * *

The Tolefson's long time friend and family doctor, Thomas Burton, had told Grace almost a year ago that her daddy was in an early stage of decline, and he was now most certainly in a moderate decline. The good doctor's prognosis was not a good one.

"We still know so little about it all, Grace," he said solemnly. "What we do know is that every person reacts differently. Every person has a different schedule of decline. Some can last years and live a normal life, carrying it right there in their back pocket. But to be honest, Grace, and I know this is hard, I think James will be in a very severe state by Christmas. You have some decisions to make, and soon I'm afraid! It's going to be a rough road!"

"Oh, Jules," she implored her daughter. "Christmas is only about nine months away. What are we going to do?"

"Pray, Mom . . . we will pray. God always has a plan. Now please hang up. I don't want you talking and driving!"

Grace was eighty-five years old, but she felt like she could still multitask just fine.

"Well, at least I'm not texting!"

She hung up and laughed out loud, picturing the look on her daughter's face. God knew she needed the laugh.

Grace was not worried about finances, and for this she was very thankful. Jim had retired from the Navy in 1968 and, not only did he have a great pension and some wonderful veterans benefits, many of which were a direct result of the Navy Cross medal earned in the Pacific, he had also gone to night school for three years, while working as a roofer, to learn the ins and outs of the stock market. From around 1975 until retirement, he had been employed by Merrill Lynch as a stock analyst.

Eventually, he became a fund manager, who handled billions of dollars in pension fund investment. He was great at it too. Big Grin had possessed a feel for the stock market, and he had made a lot of great investments on his own that paid dividends for his entire family. The Tolefsons were not rich by any means, but they were doing just fine. It was comforting for

Grace to know that she could afford the care her husband would need.

She did not put Jim into a care facility but, instead, kept him at home and hired caregivers and nurses to come in several times a day to look after his wellbeing. Soon, their job would be a full time one, for by Thanksgiving her husband had no idea who she was. He had forgotten their friends and their family. He wouldn't know a stock from a bond. He had even forgotten his beloved U.S. Navy. He needed care around the clock. It was all quite heartbreaking!

Julie and Randy had blessed Jim and Grace with two "chip off the old block" grandsons. The boys were in their twenties and both had taken more after their grandfather than their dad. Randy never thought for a minute that either boy would become a fireman, and he was right. His oldest son, Robert, had followed in his granddad's footsteps and become a pretty big deal at Goldman Sachs Corp, while the youngest, Billy, joined the Navy.

In early December both of these young men would have to make a life-altering decision and, thankfully, both of them had some help in the matter.

* * *

Bobby sat at his desk pondering over a Hong Kong investment decision. With a faltering economy and a very shaky stock market, he was looking for a company with real growth potential. He was being pressured by some pretty big corporations, and even the state government, who were seeing their pension funds begin to dwindle. He could be a real hero if he could find a company to invest in that would lift those funds out of the doldrums, and he thought he had found such a company. Hong Kong Tel seemed to control all of the telecom business in and around a good part of the Orient, and it seemed primed for some real growth and gain over the next several years. The research came out well and, at a meeting of the minds at Goldman just that morning, he had been given the go ahead to pull the trigger and to start buying up the stock.

But as he hit the computer keys to start the transaction mode he was interrupted by a voice.

"I wouldn't do that!"

Robert Tolefson turned and looked into the face of a man much younger than himself. The man (*boy?*) was dressed to the nines in a very nice suit and a very expensive tie. Bobby WOULD notice that, for he had a thing for ties.

"Who are you?" asked Bobby incredulously.

"I am Jimmy from upstairs, and I am sort of an expert around here. You don't have to listen to me, but I do urge you to check with an old friend of mine in Japan on the matter. I think this company is a failure, and I also believe they are about to re-structure their whole company. Their reports are not in order. Hong Kong Tel lies like a rug about their balance sheets, and they in point of fact could go under within days. Avoid it like the plague, son. Trust me here, Bobby. Call Yoshi Tashaki at the Japanese exchange. I guarantee he will back me on this!"

"Son???" Bobby had a strange feeling but went ahead and called the Japanese exchange and asked for Mr. Tashaki. He was immediately informed that Yoshi had been dead for years.

He turned to ask Jimmy about it, but the very well dressed young fellow was gone. It was like he just vanished. It seemed like he had never even been there at all!

For whatever reason, Bobby never pulled the trigger and the very next day the stock price of Hong Kong Tel dropped right off the chart!

* * *

Young Billy was a Gunners Mate on a destroyer that was patrolling the Straits of Hormuz in support of the Stennis Air Carrier group. He had been onboard this boat for eleven solid months, but the warship was designated to head stateside soon.

Billy Tolefson would be home by Christmas, and the thought

was comforting. Billy was known as a GM in the Ordinance Division and was in charge of all munitions aboard ship and also manned most of the weapons that were used against enemy surface ships or hostile aircraft.

So when the ship's alarms went off early that December morning, it was William Tolefson who manned the 50 caliber M240B machine gun on the starboard side of the destroyer, a destroyer not unlike his grandfather's boat in World War II.

From the time he was little, Billy's mom had told him all about the exploits of "Big Grin!" The young boy just adored his Pop Pop and knew from very early on in his life that he would one day join the Navy and try to be just like him. He hoped that one day he, William Tolefson, would command a Naval warship. But, for now, the young GM had a big problem. An enemy frigate of sorts was heading right for the destroyer. His cockles were up, and he was a bit scared. However he was locked and loaded and ready to go.

The warnings were given.

"Identify yourself or you will be fired upon."

"Change your course now or we will commence firing."

The ship kept coming. There was no visible flag or identification on the vessel.

Then Billy heard a command in his earpiece that he was not expecting to hear.

"Do not fire! Under any circumstance, do NOT fire! STAND DOWN! We do not need another incident out here."

Then Bill heard another voice. "Another INCIDENT? Like the U.S. COLE? The man is a politically correct idiot. I say fire at will!"

Billy turned and looked into the face of the youngest sailor he had ever seen. This kid could not have been much older than seventeen. How did he get up here on the turret without being seen?

The boat moved closer . . . more warnings were issued from the bridge.

"Listen, boy, your grandfather sent me. Commander James 'Big Grin' Tolefson says fire and fire right NOW!"

Billy opened fire. He gave that attacking ship all he had. As he was being screamed at in his earpiece, the enemy boat exploded with such a force that the concussion of it all rattled the big destroyer.

Billy hit his head hard and fell unconscious. When he awoke he was severely yelled at for not heeding orders, and then he was awarded the Navy Distinguished Service Medal for individually neutralizing a threat that might have, WOULD have, sunk the U.S. destroyer. This Navy DSM, with a gold star device and anchor, had never been given to a sailor of his rank and duty. NEVER in the history of the U.S. Navy!

The attack boat was later identified as an Iranian-sponsored Al-Qaeda-operated vessel packed with C4 explosives. If it had succeeded in its mission, it would have made the U.S. COLE incident in Yemen look like child's play.

* * *

So it was on Christmas morning that everyone was gathered around Jim's bed, after the attendant had left for a bit, and held hands and prayed. They asked God to bless their family on this wonderful day. They thanked God for bringing Billy safely home from the Gulf and prayed that He might look after Jim.

"In this life and in the next," prayed Grace. "Let's all go downstairs and eat!"

The Tolefsons gathered around the dinner table as they had done for years. There was an empty chair at the head of the table to honor Jim. There was Grace, Julie and Randy, and their two sons, Robert and William.

The food was scrumptious as usual. Grace ALWAYS went all out for Christmas dinner. Renee and Carter had stopped by early that morning to visit Jim and drop off some of Renee's special squash casserole, which was wonderful . . . as if they needed any more food.

It was a blessed time, yet a very sad time, as Jim lay

upstairs in his bed oblivious to all that was going on downstairs. The boys were talking a mile a minute about the miracles in their lives when yet another miracle took place!

Penelope Campbell let herself into the house and quietly passed by the Tolefson's dinner table. She had worked with hospice and various assisted living services for over ten years now. She was a very dedicated woman and was, therefore, very anxious to get back to her duties.

"Hello, Penny, are you hungry?" asked Grace. "I thought you would be gone a bit longer."

"No, Ms. Grace. And no, ma'am." I ate a bunch at home and spent some quality time with my family on this wonderful Christmas morning, which was much appreciated. But I had to get back to Mr. Jim."

"Okay, well, yell if you need something," answered Ms. Grace.

Within a few moments Penelope needed something. She came running down the steps with what looked like a letter in her hand! She was waving it back and forth and yelling hysterically.

Being the first responder that he was, Randy jumped up first and ran towards Penny, who had stopped at the bottom of the stairs and was panting and talking all at once.

She handed Randy the letter.

"This is impossible, Mr. Jim is still in his bed, but this freshly-written letter was sitting on the top of the old antique desk. The chair was even pulled out."

She might have fainted right there had Randy not had her in his grasp.

"Here, Mom," said Randy, as he handed the letter to Grace and then proceeded to get Penny a glass of water.

"It's not possible . . . just not possible . . ." Penny said over and over, but regaining some composure, she continued. "I'm going back up and leave you alone."

She ascended the stairs still muttering in sort of a whispered tone. She may have been praying. It was hard to tell.

Everyone set back down and Grace began to read the letter.

"It reads, to my beloved family." Grace looked up for a second in disbelief and then plowed onwards.

"I am not sure how much longer I have here, so I would like to say a few things from my heart on this blessed Christmas Day. First of all, I love every single one of you and I am also very proud of you.

"Bobby, it is a noble work that you are doing. Your investment wisdom will, in turn, affect so many people. Regular working stiffs who will one day have a bit of a nest egg to lean upon because of you. Never lose sight of that fact . . . and you were right about that Hong Kong Company."

Robert knew at that moment that Jimmy from upstairs had been his grandfather. He really might have known it all along.

"And that girlfriend of yours, Melinda? Marry that girl, Robert. She is a good one and they are hard to find!"

Bobby had only been dating Melinda for about six months and didn't really know that Pop Pop had any idea about the relationship. His face reddened a bit as Billy giggled out loud.

Grace continued to read.

"Billy, my boy. You're a Navy man after my own heart. I am proud of you, son. That boat SHOULD have been blown out of the water. Your CO and XO had a rock in their heads at the wrong moment. This political correctness baloney has no place in war, son. That whole ship would have gone down if not for you! You will command a boat like that one day, and YOU will know better."

It was then that young Gunnery Mate William Tolefson understood that it was his Pop Pop who had helped him man that 50 caliber on that day. He wasn't sure how that was possible . . . yet he just KNEW!

"My daughter . . ." Grace continued on. "I love you more than life itself. Always have. God loves you too. You are a good woman who has spent a lifetime loving and caring for God's creatures. Each one matters to Him, Peaches. Just as you matter to me. I have always been so very proud of you. You have always meant everything to me . . . my Julie . . . ARGGH!"

Julie was overcome with emotion. She put her face in her hands. "Oh, Daddy . . . my daddy," she cried.

"You, Randy Stinson, have been a wonderful husband to my daughter. Plus, you have given a lifetime of service to humanity itself, risking life and limb time and time again to rescue people from harm. These things do not go unnoticed. You may be the best of all of us!"

"Thank you, sir," Randy whispered.

"Grace, my love . . . my precious wife."

Grace broke down at this point and handed the letter to her oldest grandson, who finished reading it for her.

"I know how hard this has all been on you," Bobby read. "It's been much tougher on you than on me, my love. My times of darkness and frustration have melted away every time I heard your sweet voice talking to me. Yes . . . somewhere in my head and heart I heard every word. Memory is a treasure, my dear, and you and this family have provided me with great memories that I HAVE managed to hold on to. From deep in the darkness I am always looking for a light, and that light is YOU, my Grace. Our eternal love . . . one for the other . . . well, I can assure you . . . it will never die.

"I have one more thing to say. God is real . . . Heaven is real . . . the Angels are real. I have been with them. I have sat at the very feet of Jesus Christ, and His message is Love and Light, Forgiveness and LIFE for those of us who believe in Him. He has gone to prepare a place for us, which is far away from war and politics and sickness like Alzheimer's.

"We will gather again one day, just as we are now and worship Him and thank Him for the miracles of this day and EVERYDAY."

The letter came to end right there. There was no signature . . . not that one was needed.

"How did this happen, Mom?" asked Julie. "How did he do it? How COULD he have done this?"

"It is Christmas, Julie . . . a day of miracles. I think the answer is as plain and simple as that. I believe one of his angels must have helped him write it. Yes, I do!"

It was then that Penny called to them a second time. Her hysteria had been replaced by her usual calm and professional manner.

Grace, Julie, Randy, Robert, and William somberly walked up the steps and into the master bedroom. Jim was in his bed. He was just as silent and still as he had ever been.

"His breathing accelerated and then all of a sudden he was hardly breathing at all. I thought you all should come. I think this may be the end." Penny said quietly, as she moved back and let Grace, Julie, Randy, Bobby, and Billy gather around the bed.

Grace took his hand and quietly prayed. Then she spoke.

"You thanked us for providing good memories for you to cling upon in the darkness. Well, dear husband, I thank YOU for all of the great memories and love that you have provided for all of us. You have been a good man. A spiritual man. A brave man. And we have all leaned upon you all of these years.

"Lean on us now, dear one, and go on home. Go on home, my husband, my love . . . Tell Jesus I'll be along shortly and ask those angels of yours to look over all of us until that reunion of which you spoke. I will thank and praise God forever for allowing you to visit us one more time on this Christmas Day. Such a miracle . . . such a miracle . . ."

With his family all around him, Commander James "Big Grin" Tolefson U.S.N. let go of his last breath and went home to the Savior.

He was smiling. . .

Authors note: A special thank you to Duane Allen for his insight in dealing with Alzheimer's and the importance of providing good memories for one to hold on to . . . (JSB)

Little Jerry's Christmas

Little Jerry was ten years old and very, very unhappy. He could hear his mother crying in the other room, and he just hated to see her feeling sad. It always made him feel sad, as well. Of course, it was his father's fault, as usual, and that made it worse.

On top of it all, it was Christmas Eve, a time when everyone should be happier. Earlier that day little Jerry and his mom had walked over to the old used car lot on Sampson Street, where they bought a pretty cool tree from old man Haggerty. Mr. Haggerty sold trees every year. Most of the neighborhood families bought their trees there. It was tradition.

In Jerry's opinion, it was a darn good thing Haggerty sold trees at Christmastime because hardly anyone ever bought a car from the guy. It seemed the same old cars and trucks were sitting there all year long. He knew Emily Haggerty quite well. She was in his class at school, and he could tell she didn't have very much. But . . . who did?

Jerry and his mother had dragged the tree on home, retrieved the old stand and decorations from the basement, and put it up in a corner of the living room. It looked great, too. Lots of blinking lights, tinsel, balls of all kinds, and the most wonderful, white angel on the very top of the tree.

The angel seemed to look right at you no matter where you stood. Little Jerry loved that beautiful angel. Mom had had it for as long as he could remember. In actuality, she had had that angel since her own childhood.

There was also a small manger scene that Jerry's mom always put at the foot of the tree. She said it was so they would "never forget the real meaning of Christmas!" It had a place for one bright light in the back and, when lit up, the Baby Jesus would shine. It was very cool!

Jerry lay in his bed, stared out of the back window, and thought of his father. He didn't exactly hate Big Jerry, but sometimes he didn't like him very much at all. His mother had explained to him over and over that his father was different than most men because he fought in a war. Then she always added that 'he was a good man, a hard working provider for the family, and he loved us all very much!'

Well, sometimes it was hard for little Jerry to reconcile all of this and place "good man" in the same thought pattern with the stumbling drunk who entered the house about once a week. His mom called them "binges!"

Sometimes his dad was just fine for a long time. He would come home at night, eat dinner, be nice to him and his mom, go to bed and get up early the next morning and head for the factory. Big Jerry did work hard for a living. There was never a doubt about that. He was a maintenance man and electrician, and he was a very valuable employee at whatever firm he worked. But a bad "binge" could bring on a rapid change in employment from time to time.

One never knew when this would happen. All of a sudden, a given Friday would come around and Jerry's dad just didn't come home. Sometimes he was only gone for the weekend, but other times he was gone for weeks. That was when Big Jerry had to find a new job and a new boss . . . and a new paycheck!

On occasion Jerry's mom would cut a binge short by sending her son out on a search mission. Little Jerry would board his bike and cruise all over the northeast part of the city looking for his father. The kid knew where just about every bar was located, which was really something, as there seemed to be a "tavern" on every other corner.

Once he found Big Jerry, usually slumped down low and drunk on a barstool, at some place called the Shamrock or whatever the place might be called, the kid would pedal hard for home and "rat out" his dad's present location. Then, a call would go out to one or two of the men in the neighborhood to "go and get him!"

And they would. It was not very pretty or very inspiring.

As he was on this Christmas Eve, Jerry would always lie in his room, stare at the ceiling, and wonder which drunk would come home this time. There were actually three. The 'funny drunk,' who would be laughing and making jokes until he collapsed into a coma, the 'mean drunk,' who was like a miserable time bomb that could do a lot of damage to a wall or a door or even his wife or son. Then there was what the boy referred to as the 'sad, army guy drunk.' This drunk was perhaps the most bothersome of all, because on some level he broke down all of little Jerry's shields of defense.

It was easy to ignore the funny drunk and easy to hate the mean drunk. But the sad, army drunk just broke little Jerry's heart. His father, who would smell of beer mixed with cheap whiskey, cigarettes and Hershey bars, just sat and wept like a little boy. He would hug his son and tell him he was sorry for all of his shortcomings. He would hint at the fact that he had lost some good friends in the war and that they were heroes. He said it should have been him who was killed in that explosion.

Eventually, his mom would help Big Jerry to bed and once there, she would cradle him like a little boy, sing to him . . . and pray for him.

His mom had explained to the boy over and over that his father was that way because of the war and that little Jerry should never give up on him for no matter what, "He IS your FATHER!"

The boy was not stupid. He could see that somewhere along the way his father had suffered a great sadness, and fighting in a war had to be just awful. But in little Jerry's opinion it was "still no good reason to act like a jerk!"

And besides, it was CHRISTMAS! The tree was all lit up and his father was in some bar drinking boilermakers. It was just not right!

Then little Jerry began to hear a low murmuring sound emanating from up the hall. It seemed like someone was whispering. He crawled out of bed and, catlike, crept down the hallway and put his ear against the front bedroom door that was shared by his parents. The voice he heard was his mom. She was praying. As long as the boy would live, he would never forget his mother's words on that Christmas Eve.

Dear Precious and Heavenly Father, I ask you tonight to look after my husband. He IS a good man, and he has suffered greatly and been through so much. I pray tonight, Heavenly Father, that on this Christmas Eve you might see fit to bless him and forgive him and love him. And if it be Thy will, bring him home to this house—and to me and to his son, who DO love him so very much. We need him here, oh Lord, and he needs YOU, in his heart and in his life. You are the Master of all, and You have said in Your Word that You would lift our heavy burdens. Well, Lord, I just cannot take much more.

Please, God, make him stop drinking. Help him to live with the deaths of those other soldiers and be the husband and father he should be. God, I know You are able to do this and, on this night when many years ago, You saw fit to give us Your only, precious Son. I thought perhaps you might have mercy on a mother and HER son who really need a blessing. But only if it be Your will. Thank you . . . in Jesus name. Amen.

Little Jerry wiped the tears that were streaming down his own face, crept back down the hall, and then went downstairs to the living room. He sat on the couch and stared up at the angel, who was perched at the very top of the tree in all of his lit up glory.

He noted that there were no presents beneath the tree as of yet, but there would be a few there by morning. His mom always went to work around Christmas so they could afford some presents under the tree. His mom always waited until little Jerry was fast asleep and put the gifts under the tree before the sun came up. Jerry figured she always ate the cookies and drank the milk that he had set out for Santa the night before, but he never let her know that he knew!

The angel seemed to stare at the boy as it always did. Little Jerry stared right back. After awhile the boy found himself speaking to the beautiful ornament that lived in a box behind the tool shed for fifty-one weeks of the year. He felt a little dumb but . . . why not?

"Mister Angel," the boy whispered. "I know that there are

angels for real. My mom taught me that they are everywhere and that each of us has a special one just to watch over us kids. So, if it is not too much trouble, could you please speak to God and ask Him to answer my mom's prayers tonight? Please bring my father home, ummmm, sober, if that's okay. Also, please tell God that I love Him, too, and I thank Him for Baby Jesus. Amen."

And with that . . . little Jerry went back upstairs, curled beneath his covers, and fell into a very deep sleep.

* * *

Big Jerry, as usual, was feeling sad and alone. He sat at the end of the bar and ordered another round. A tall draft beer and a shot of Four Roses to go with it. This was about his fifth boilermaker of the night, and he was already starting to feel a bit better.

But soon that would change. It was always this way.

A range of alcohol-induced emotions always culminated in a bad ending. A drunk and dark hole from which there seemed no escape. Visions of young men in a desert, laughing and smoking cigarettes, and then something slipped. They were all gone . . . but him.

Big Jerry could just not come to grips with these visions, so he drank until he passed out, usually asking God for forgiveness.

"Forgiveness? For what?" asked the tall blond-haired man in

what seemed to be a white or cream colored suit and tie, who now occupied the bar stool beside Jerry.

Big Jerry's head had been bowed down low. His forehead almost touching the end of the bar when he heard the voice of the man seated beside him.

He rose up and looked into a pair of deep, dark blue eyes, the likes of which he had never seen in his life, and answered.

"Forgiveness . . . for just being alive," he slurred.

"Life is a great gift, Jerry," the man answered. "It is not your fault that Sergeant Briscoe and Private First Class Benton are not here today. That was NOT your decision to make, you know."

"But I could have . . . "

"Could have what, Jerry? You were a few yards away getting ammo when the mortar hit. It is all just simple as that! The world revolves. Things happen. We turn left or we turn right. We go up. We go down. We live . . . we die.

"There was nothing you could have done that day." He continued, "The war was hard enough with all the killing and death everywhere. No reason to keep blaming yourself for something you had no control over."

"But . . . Sir . . . I . . . " murmured Big Jerry.

"Get in the ball game, soldier, you have a precious wife and son at home right now who love you. And need you. Besides, it is CHRISTMAS. Sober up, man . . . and that is an order."

Big Jerry began to feel his head clear up. His whole body began to tremble and shake, and he began to weep uncontrollably.

After pulling himself together a bit, he again looked into the deep, blue eyes of the impeccably-dressed man on the next stool and asked softly, "Who ARE you, Sir"

"I am just another soldier as well, Jerry, and by the authority of HE, Who sent me to this wretched and foul smelling place . . . HE, Who holds the universe in the palm of His hand . . . HE, Who holds the keys of life and death . . . HE, Who was born of a virgin on this very day, two thousand years ago and died on a cross for YOU, Jerry. By HIS authority, I plead with you to get your act together and go home to your family, to seek the will of Jesus Christ in your life and to quit all of this drinking and feeling sorry for yourself. Be the man He wants you to be. It IS possible to do this, Jerry, I assure you. Have faith in Him. Accept CHRIST into your heart and life as your Savior and go home! Go before you lose it all. Merry Christmas, Jerry."

Jerry again seemed to lift his head from the edge of the bar and found that the man was gone.

"Hey, Marty," Jerry yelled to the bartender and the proprietor of Marty's Bar and Grill on Blake Street. "Did you get the name of that man in the fancy suit?"

"What man?" Marty asked. "Only you and me in this place tonight, and we are both about to be gone, because I am closing 'er up and going to the house."

"Never mind," answered Big Jerry as he put on his jacket and headed for the door. There seemed to be a new purpose in his being and a fresh spring in his step that did not go unnoticed by the bartender.

"Hey, big guy, how did you sober up so quick?" asked Marty who was in the process of cashing out the register behind the bar. "A minute ago you were comatose, man. Anyhow, Merry Christmas."

"Yeah, Merry Christmas, Marty."

Big Jerry ran out of Marty's Bar and Grill and headed towards home. But first he had a few stops to make.

* * *

Little Jerry was awakened by the sound of Christmas music. Ahhhhhh, another tradition. His mom always played music in order to wake him up on Christmas morning. He could hear Elvis singing "White Christmas" in the living room downstairs. But there was another sound, a mechanical sound of sorts. The boy leapt out of bed and ran downstairs taking the steps two at a time. When he reached the downstairs landing he stopped short and stared at a miracle. He could not believe what he was seeing.

There was a wooden platform that took up almost the entire living room, and there was a lit up city built upon the platform with trains going in circles, and lights blinking on and off, and little people walking down little streets and . . . it was like magic.

The tree was off to the side of the platform, and there were presents galore around the bottom, all wrapped up in the prettiest papers and bows that little Jerry had ever seen. But best of all, his father stood there, tall and proud with one arm around his mom's shoulder, and he was smiling at his son.

He then knelt down and spread his arms wide and received a running little boy full into his arms. Big Jerry tightly hugged his son and said, "Merry Christmas . . . I am home now. God has forgiven me and so has your mother. I vow to you, son, in the name of Jesus Christ, I will never drink again. We are going to be okay from here on in . . . I promise. I love you, son!!"

Little Jerry first looked at his mom, who was smiling and weeping, and then he glanced back at his dad . . . the GOOD man. The sober one.

Then he looked up into the face of the angel, who stood on top of the tree all lit up, dressed in white, blue eyes glowing beneath his blond locks and whispered two words . . .

"Thank you!"

MERRY CHRISTMAS. (JSB)

☆

Private Bluegrass: A Christmas Story

Private First Class Billy Mellon of Glasgow, Kentucky, was stationed at Fort Liberty in Baghdad, Iraq, as part of the U. S. Army 4th Infantry Division. He had been overseas for close to eighteen months serving America as a vital cog in the wheel of Operation Iraqi Freedom. He had been a part of building sewerage systems, schools and electrical plants, as well as taking part in the capture or eradication of insurgent radical Islamist terrorists. Billy and his fellow soldiers fought these terrorists in the streets, farmlands and deserts of four provinces: Baghdad, Babil, Karbala and Najaf—and the battles were far from over.

It seemed that everyone in the Army had a nickname and in Billy's case his buddies referred to him as Private Bluegrass, or the short version . . . Bluegrass! There was a good reason for the said moniker. Aside from the Army and a few short but sweet romantic interests, the twenty-year-old, light assault infantryman's entire life revolved around bluegrass music. He had played guitar and banjo since he was a little boy growing up on the Mellon family's eighty-acre, tobacco farm that was located just a bit south of Glasgow on the road to Tompkinsville.

Billy figured, when his stint in the service came to an end, he would try to make a living with strings. Many times after a tough day routing out insurgents and dodging rocket propelled grenades, Billy would lie in his bunk and picture himself "pickin' banjer" in Rhonda Vincent's band, or perhaps playing acoustic guitar and singing high harmony with the Grascals or Mountainheart.

Before joining up with Uncle Sam a few years back, Billy did some pickin' with a few local bands in Kentucky, but most of his musical experience came from sitting on the front porch with his dad in the early evenings. They would pick and sing old Bill Monroe and Flatt and Scruggs tunes together long after the sun went down, usually with his father on guitar and Billy on banjo.

Private Bluegrass could really pick and that was a fact. Last Christmas, the Glasgow Lions Club had sent Billy an old Deering Goodtime Banjo. The instrument was broken in two places and the strings were really dead and old but, when the time was right, Billy would pick on that thing for the entire division. He almost made the old banjo sound brand new. Billy owned a much nicer, Deering Sierra model at home. He was looking forward to playing it again!

Bluegrass was quite the young man. He was a darn good soldier, too—the kind of man one wanted standing beside of him when things got dicey. He was a strong and tough kid who cared about America, freedom, protection and family.

Billy's immediate family only consisted of three people. His father Jake Mellon was a big strapping kind of guy who not only raised the tobacco and grew some corn on the old farm but also worked full time for a roofing company. His mom, Lila, was the absolute sweetest woman on earth and perhaps the finest cook in the whole state. Then, of course, there was Billy, the only child of Jake and Lila who, like his dad before him, now proudly served in the United States Army.

Jake had served in Viet Nam and his Army picture had hung in the hallway at home for as long as Billy could remember. Jake never talked about the war in Southeast Asia, but his Purple Heart and Bronze Star in the desk drawer spoke volumes about his experience there. Billy always thought of his dad as a true American hero and wanted to be just like him.

Now serving in Iraq, young Billy had accomplished just that. He had become his father for certain, and in so doing, he now possessed a better understanding of Jake then ever before. A good, hardworking and patriotic man, who loved his family, loved his farm and loved his country. Even though the good old U. S. of A. had let him down a bit after he came home from Nam, Jake got over all of that and now proudly flew the Stars and Stripes in his front yard. He was proud of his time spent in country, and he was also very proud of his son for joining up to serve America, as he had done in the late sixties.

Billy found it hard to believe that he was approaching his second Christmas away from home. Billy so loved Christmas. His boyhood memories of growing up in Kentucky sometimes seemed so far away and removed from the nightmare world where he now resided most days. But he could still easily conjure up visions of Christmas mornings at the farm. The big, freshly cut fir tree. The decorations and lights his Mom kept in boxes in the barn attic for most of the year that would now illuminate the entire house. The smell of Christmas dinner, the neighbors, and even preacher Jones from the Baptist church, stopping by to visit and having a piece of one of Lila's freshly baked pies.

Then there were the special presents that were just for him. Wrapped in pretty paper and bows, they waited beneath the great tree for little Billy to run down the stairs on Christmas morning and open. These were such happy memories for the young soldier. How he wished he were home right now waiting for that magical Christmas morning to arrive.

Many times Billy would finger his Army-issued, M-4 Carbine weapon complete with lasers and a night vision scope and think back to that first Browning 22 caliber rifle his dad had placed under the beautiful Christmas tree when he was just ten years old. Billy absolutely loved that rifle. It still rested in a hallowed corner of the closet in his bedroom.

The best Christmas memories of all, though, had to be the variety of smells that permeated the house. The turkey, the freshly baked pumpkin pie, the cookies, and then there was the smell of the tree itself, which seemed to just overwhelm the entire house with its sweet aroma.

Billy was daydreaming about the smell of the fir tree when a staff sergeant by the name of Bingham called out to him and interrupted his thought pattern.

"Hey, Bluegrass, got a package for ya kid. Come on over here!"

It was just a few days before Christmas and many of the guys were receiving gifts from home. Billy knew the package was coming, because he had received an email about it from his mom a few days ago. It was cool that servicemen and women could get access to emails from home, and Billy took advantage of that when he had the chance. Lila had an Apple computer and had learned how to use email, but Jake never touched the thing. The thought made Billy smile as he ran towards Sergeant Bingham and retrieved his Christmas package from Glasgow, Kentucky.

"Thanks, Sarge," he said.

"You betcha, kid, gotta love the Army. They can get a package from Kentucky to Bedrock, but can't find Osama," laughed Bingham. "By the way, Bluegrass, new orders coming in as well. Big doings coming down on Christmas Eve, so get psyched man."

"What's up?" asked Billy.

"Best of my knowledge we are taking a heavy convoy into Tikrit on the morning of the 24th. Gonna come down heavy on some bad guys. We have good Intel on this one, too. I hear there are a few Al-Qaeda boys in the bunch. Should be a good fight . . . Merry Christmas!"

"Yeah, Sarge," answered Billy. "Same back atcha."

Billy rushed back to his makeshift barracks to open his package. He was trying not to think about the orders for the 24th. He had learned long ago not to bog himself down worrying about what was to come. You relied on your training and your buddies to do the right thing and get the job done with as few casualties as possible. He would be there, as usual, on the front line of the war on terror, and he WOULD do his job.

America counted on him and he would not let her down.

Billy stood in line for well over two hours waiting for his turn at the computer. He finally sat down and wrote a short email to his mom. It read in part: Thanks so much for the candy bars, the underwear and the cookies, but thanks a million for the iPod, Mom. This is HUGE! I have to find out how you did it. There are over a thousand songs on here. THANK YOU, THANK YOU and THANK YOU some more! Please give Dad a big hug for me, too. I miss you both so very much. Keep me in your prayers, Mom, and God bless you both. Merry Christmas! I love you dearly, Billy.

The iPod was chock full of bluegrass songs by every artist imaginable, from Ricky Skaggs and Kentucky Thunder to Bill Monroe and Alison Krauss. His mom had even sent a USB connector so he could plug the iPod into a computer and charge it up from time to time.

This was the greatest gift he could have ever received. *"How in the world did she ever get this done?"* Billy continued to ponder.

The evening of December 23rd found Billy in his bunk reading his Bible and listening to Jim Mills play banjo on his iPod. His mom knew that Mills was his favorite modern day banjo player. Billy eventually fell asleep and dreamed about the big tree in the living room at home. His father was sitting in his favorite chair softly picking his old Martin guitar and his sweet mother was in the kitchen baking.

Private First Class William Mellon, also known as Private Bluegrass, would be shipping out early the next morning for the very dangerous town of Tikrit. *"Should be a good fight,"* he thought, echoing Sergeant Bingham, as the sound of Jim Mills banjo version of "Standing In The Need Of Prayer" pounded through the tiny ear buds of his brand new iPod.

About the same time, just south of Glasgow, Kentucky, Lila Mellon logged out of her Yahoo email account and shut down the MacBook Pro laptop her husband had bought her as a birthday gift. She made her way back to the kitchen area of the humble farmhouse where she and Jake resided, joining the man she had loved and adored since her senior year of high school at the table. Jake was reading the latest issue of the Tompkinsville Gazette.

"Billy received his package with the iPod," whispered Lila. "He is one happy camper!"

Jake looked up and smiled at his loving wife. "I miss my son," he said softly.

"So do I, honey!"

She reached across the table and grasped both of Jake's hardworking hands in her own and shut her eyes.

"Say a prayer, Jake. Say a prayer for Billy."

Jake closed his eyes and began to speak softly and humbly.

"Dear Precious and Heavenly Father. I am a simple man, and I do not claim to know how or why things happen as they do, but I want you to know that I love you, Lord. As always, my wife and I pray that your will be done in all things concerning this family. We do ask, in all humility, to watch over our son. Protect him, Lord, and bless him as he and his friends serve you and serve this nation in a dangerous corner of the world. I know it is a lot to ask but, if you can see your way clear to even consider it, please send him home to us this Christmas . . . Amen."

Jake had to stop speaking. He was overcome with emotion at his own words. He rose up from the table and took Lila in his arms and held her. They both wept like little children.

At 0500 the following morning Billy found himself standing in a long line of young men and women who shared a common goal. They were stoked and ready for whatever the day might bring. They would follow their orders and fight the enemies of the free world. They were prepared to die if necessary for this cause and, no doubt, some of them would indeed not see the evening sunset. Their convoy of Humvees would plow into Tikrit and rendezvous at an appointed destination, and the battle would begin. As in so many times past, Billy would whisper a silent prayer asking the Lord for protection for he and his comrades. He would humbly ask for a successful mission and would always add, "Nevertheless, Thy will be done," as his mother had taught him to pray so many years ago. Billy was about to enter the shotgun seat of the lead Humvee when he heard the coarse voice of his commanding officer.

"Private First Class Mellon, front and center, soldier. And I mean right now!"

Billy jumped to attention, while at the same time wondering just why in the world the CO was calling his name.

The answer came immediately.

"The President and the Pentagon have decided to send one hundred soldiers home for Christmas. Names were drawn from a hat and your name was one of them. You are going home, son."

Billy's heart jumped. *"What?"*

"But, Sir, with all due respect we have this mission and . . . "

"You have no choice in the matter, soldier," answered the CO. "Pack light, because you are coming right back after Christmas!"

"Sir, I just do not understand this, I mean, I am grateful and all, and I would love to go home. But I can't leave my friends in a lurch here. I mean I have to . . . "

"Private, the U. S. Army will get along just fine over here without you. Now be on board that transport to the airport by

0600 hours. That is a direct order. One day to get home, one day there and one day to get your behind back to Baghdad. That is all!"

It was a miracle of gigantic proportions. Private Bluegrass was now on his way home to Glasgow, Kentucky, while the rest of his division made their way to Tikrit. On this Christmas Eve morning those soldiers would come face to face with one of the toughest and perhaps the bloodiest battle of the entire war.

So it was around noon on Christmas day when Billy Mellon walked down the long gravel driveway towards the home of his childhood. His mother Lila was in the kitchen removing a pumpkin pie from the oven and Jake was sitting in the living room by the tree watching Jimmy Stewart on the television. Although he had seen Clarence get his wings a million times, he still always fought back a tear when the bells on the tree began to ring. *Every time a bell rings an angel gets his . . .*

"JAKE, OH JAKE! Come here! It's BILLY! It's BILLY!"

Jake Mellon immediately jumped three feet in the air and right out of his chair in response to the sound of his screaming wife. Without even thinking he found himself running towards the front door, beating Lila there by about a step and a half. When he threw the door open he nearly tore the thing off its hinges.

Within seconds he was holding his only son deep within

his arms. With tears welling up in his eyes he finally backed away from the boy and let his wife repeat the procedure. Lila was also crying as she hugged her Billy and proceeded to rock him back and forth as if he were five years old and had just arrived home with a skinned up knee after a romp in the woods.

Lila began to giddily talk like a cartoon character.

"Oh Billy, why are you home? What a shock . . . what a surprise . . . I hope we have enough food . . . I only prepared for me and your father. Oh, sweet Jesus . . . there are no presents under the tree for you . . . we didn't expect . . . praise His Holy Name . . . I . . ."

She near fell over and might have had Jake not grabbed her arm and held on to it.

"Mom, Dad, it is okay, really," said Billy just now putting down his lightly packed duffel bag. "I am only here for a day. They picked my name out of a hat and anyway . . . I go back to Iraq tomorrow."

Jake picked up the boy's bag in his meaty hand and said, "Then let us enjoy this blessed day with our son. I will take this up to your room, Billy. It hasn't changed a bit since you left home."

Billy followed his father up the stairs, leaving Lila standing there by the still open front door. She was mumbling and praying at the same time, but Jake figured she would be okay soon, and he was right.

Lila had plenty of food. She had prepared a beautiful turkey, fresh corn, green beans, cranberries, mashed potatoes and plenty of gravy. Then came the pies. There were three to choose from . . . pumpkin, apple, and raspberry. Billy ate a small piece of each one.

He had only dreamed of a meal such as this while in Afghanistan and then Iraq. *There was enough here to feed an army. Well, an Army of One, anyway.*

He laughed at the thought. This whole experience seemed surreal to Billy. It was like a dream. How very sweet to be home on the farm with his mom and dad on Christmas day. How very sweet indeed.

The sun goes down early in Kentucky around December 25th, and the early evening found Billy and his dad sitting in the living room with a banjo and guitar in hand. They didn't say a word for almost two hours. They just picked song after song as they had always done. Lila sat on the couch and took it all in. The two men is her life, sitting together, playing and singing. This was as it should be, and she was so very thankful.

Billy did not want to talk about the war, and Jake did not push the matter. During a break in the music, however, Billy said, "They call me Private Bluegrass!"

Jake smiled and Lila asked, "What if you get a promotion?"

"I guess I would be Corporal Bluegrass," answered Billy.

Jake saw an opening. "How tough is it over there, son?"

"Pretty tough, Dad, but not like you keep seeing on the news. We are doing a lot of good. I am proud of all those who are serving. The big problem is not knowing who the enemy is. You learn to trust somebody. Then, next thing you know, that guy you thought you knew drives up in a car and 'boom.' Everything blows. People die!" Billy's voice trailed off a bit.

"Been there, son. Sounds like Nam!"

"Just keep praying for us guys. We are going to win this thing with God's help."

"We never stop praying for you, son," said Lila.

"I know, Mom. I love you both so much. This has been such a blessing to be here with you both, even for this short time. It is the greatest Christmas gift a soldier could ever receive."

Billy put the banjo in its case and continued, "I am so tired, I think I will head up to my room and hit the sack."

He hugged his mom and dad and slowly walked up the stairs to his bedroom carrying his banjo case. It was a beautiful sight. At the top of the stairs Billy turned and smiled. To her dying day, Lila would always remember that smile.

Lila and Jake's bedroom was on the first floor, and very soon after they heard Billy's door softly close upstairs, they went on to bed as well. This had been a very emotional day and the Mellon family was just exhausted.

Jake woke up with the sun as he always did. He proceeded

to the kitchen and cranked up the coffee pot. As he poured his first cup of Folgers his eye caught some movement in the driveway. A car was pulling up in front of the house. It seemed to be a rather official looking car at that.

Police? Government?

Three men got out of the car and proceeded up the stone steps to the front door. Sheriff Bentley was one of the men. Reverend Jones was there and the third man wore the unmistakable uniform of the United States Army. Jake did not know this man, and the sight of all those medals hanging there on his chest made his blood run cold.

Something was wrong. *Had Billy done something wrong? Was he A.W.O.L.? Or worse? Had he committed a crime?*

The soft knock on the door shook Jake out of his present thought pattern. *Why such a soft knock?*

Lila appeared at his side in her housecoat as he opened the door. She instinctively held on to his arm as the three men entered the house and took a seat in the living room.

Lila and Jake sat down as well. The lights on the tree continued to blink. The little red and green and white bulbs seemed oblivious to the darkening mood that began to permeate the air of the Mellon home.

The sheriff and preacher continued to say absolutely nothing at all, but their expressions spoke volumes.

This was going to be bad, thought Jake. Things seemed to be moving in slow motion. Although the men had only been inside the house for a minute or so, it was beginning to seem like they had been there for hours.

"Mr. and Mrs. Mellon, I am Lieutenant Colonel Franklin Bell. I am sorry to tell you that your son Private First Class William Mellon was killed in action yesterday in the city of Tikrit in Iraq. I am so sorry."

Jake and Lila were stunned.

Bell continued. "Your son is a hero. I have brought you this commendation, and I am honored yet saddened to present you with this Purple Heart and Bronze Star. May God bless and comfort you both."

"I am so sorry, Jake," said the sheriff rising from his chair.

"I am here for you both if you need me," said the preacher.

Bell stood and continued, "You son's body will be shipped home in a few days. He has earned the right to be buried at Arlington National Cemetery. I will be glad to help with . . . "

Lila finally stood straight up and interrupted the highly decorated Lieutenant Colonel.

"This is ridiculous, preposterous and beyond words. What is wrong with you people? My son is alive. He is here in this house. He is, in fact, upstairs in his bed as we speak!"

Jake was still feeling a chill in his bones as he walked up the stairs. He proceeded down the hall and opened the door to

Billy's room. He proceeded to feel even colder as he opened the door and stared at the empty bed. Billy was not in bed. Billy was not in the room. Billy was not anywhere in the house. There was no sign that he had ever been there.

The banjo was in its case and leaning against the wall by the bed, just as it had been before last night's picking circle. The small duffel bag was nowhere to be seen. The bed seemed just as untouched as it had been for the previous eighteen months Billy had been overseas.

Lila Mellon fainted dead out on the floor of the empty bedroom.

Long after the three men had left. Lila and Billy sat in silence on the living room couch. They were bewildered and shaken and by now all cried out, although many tears would be shed over the next few weeks and beyond.

Jake turned on the lamp, put on his reading glasses and began to carefully unfold the piece of paper that had been presented with the two medals. The commendation was actually in the form of a personal letter.

He began to softly read the words to his wife.

My Dear Mr. and Mrs. Mellon:
 On December 24, 2006, Private First Class William Mellon's unit was ambushed in the town of Tikrit. The Humvee in which he was riding was hit broadside by a rocket propelled grenade, which killed two soldiers and wounded three others including PFC Mellon. A bloody

battle ensued with armed insurgents that lasted over four hours. With complete disregard to his own injuries, Mellon dragged the wounded soldiers, one by one, to the safety of a building, all the while answering the enemy with small arms fire. Most of his unit was pinned down behind their Humvees. After ascertaining where the heaviest fire was coming from, Mellon on his own initiative proceeded to attack the position. Utilizing grenades and his M-4 Carbine, he managed to kill twelve insurgents, thereby, compromising their position and softening the attack long enough to allow his division to move forward and overcome the enemy.

Seven U.S. soldiers paid the ultimate price in this battle, including PFC Mellon, who unfortunately succumbed due to the severity of his wounds. I am saddened and sorry for the loss of such a fine soldier. I wish I knew the right words to say, but there are no words that can comfort a mother and father in a time like this.

On behalf of the United States Army and the President of the United States, I thank you for this soldier. He was among the best of us. I am so sorry for this immeasurable loss. May God bless and comfort you both on this day.

General Robert F. Girard
Fort Liberty, Iraq

PS: The men all loved him. They called him Private Bluegrass. He was a good man.

Jake passed the letter and the two medals to Lila. She read over the letter and held the two medals close to her heart.

"I am so bewildered, my dear husband. He was here. I know he was here. We could not have imagined this."

"Lila, he WAS here. I believe his presence in this house was a Christmas gift from the Heavenly Father who knows and understands our hearts much better than we do. God heard our prayer around the table a few nights ago and saw fit to send Billy home to us for Christmas. I will be grateful to Him for the rest of my life for giving us this miracle."

Lila nodded in agreement, however she was still brokenhearted.

"Honey, listen to me," Jake went on. "Remember the first Christmas Day when Mary gave birth to a son and laid him in a manger? She and Joseph knew their little boy would one day grow up and sacrifice his own life for others. Jesus himself once said that there is no greater love then to lay down one's life for his friends. Our son was here, Lila. I believe that as much as I believe anything. Our son also sacrificed his life . . . for his friends . . . for his parents . . . and for this country."

"This is all true enough, honey, but it is so hard." Lila replied softly. "How will we ever get over this?"

Jake put his arms around his wife and held on to her for a long time.

"God will get help us through, my dear wife. So will the memory of our dear son. Although he now rests in the Everlasting Arms, his spirit will always live in this house. We will never stop missing Billy. There will always be a hole in our hearts and our lives, but we will move on. Minute by minute, day by day, and someday we will see our son again. I believe this Lila. I really do."

"I believe all of that too, Jake, but as a mother . . . I am really going to need some help."

"I know, sweetheart. I know."

Jake and Lila sat in silence for most of the day and stared at the blinking lights of the Christmas tree. Early evening began to descend upon the Mellon farm.

Lila was now fast asleep on the couch still clutching Billy's medals to her chest. Jake made himself a turkey sandwich and then slowly walked upstairs and entered the bedroom of his son. He walked over to the bed in the semidarkness and turned on the small lamp, which sat atop a piece of antique furniture that had been there since Billy was little. A lamp stand of sorts, it was made of cedar and contained one tiny drawer and two small shelves.

A Lila thing, he thought. The rest of the room was all Billy. There was not one empty space on the walls. Along with the University of Kentucky Wildcat stuff, there were old concert posters. Bill Monroe and The Bluegrass Boys . . . LIVE. Renfro Valley . . . August 8th. FLATT and SCRUGGS . . . Grand Ol' Opry . . . Tonight! See THE DEL McCOURY BAND . . . October 6th at Western Kentucky University Field House.

Then there was also a huge U. S. ARMY poster. Jake laid his head back on Billy's pillow and stared at that one for a while. Be a part of HISTORY. Join TODAY . . . The ARMY of ONE!

Indeed, he thought. How strange that his son also earned a Bronze Star and Purple Heart, just as he had done in 1966. Sometimes he could still smell the napalm, and even now both legs began to ache from the old wounds that still haunted him. That was another time and another war, but somehow he and his boy had experienced the same thing.

Except that I am still alive with the memories, he thought. *Oh God, I would happily trade places if I could!*

Without really thinking he reached over to switch off the lamp and noticed that the drawer in the lamp stand was partially open. Jake could have sworn it was closed when he had turned on the lamp.

He gently pulled the drawer open all the way and immediately his heart started to pound harder. He thought he might pass out as his wife had done in this very room a bit earlier. There in the open drawer lay Billy's iPod. The very one that Lila had sent overseas for Christmas. Some boys at church had loaded it up with about a thousand songs or more and . . . *but it was* HERE! Billy HAD been here, too.

Jake lay back down on the bed and fumbled around with the tiny piece of technology, which was for the most part way beyond his fields of expertise. However, he finally figured out how to turn the thing on and did just that. He heard the music emanating from a distance, so he placed the tiny ear buds in his ear and shut off the lamp.

Jake Mellon laid there in the darkness of the bedroom of his only son and listened to Jim Mills picking his banjo version of "Standing In The Need Of Prayer."

The big man could not hold back the tears. The battles were over for Billy Mellon.

Private Bluegrass . . . was HOME!

☆

SNOWBALL . . . A Christmas Miracle

Marissa Marie Errington was thirteen years old. She had auburn hair and wore it relatively long—as compared to the shorter hairstyles preferred by most of her peers at the Batavia School for Gifted Girls—and she relished the fact that she looked a bit different from the rest of the pack.

Marissa had always been different in many respects. First off, she had to bear the burden of being an Errington, which in and of itself caused the young girl to be a bit defensive. In fact, somewhat withdrawn. She would much rather spend her time away from people, living in her own little world of make believe and music and such, than to discuss her parents and answer inane questions. Questions like, "Oh, wow, what is it really like to have the great Robert Errington as a father, or the much loved and respected Donna Errington as a mother?"

It had been like that since she was a young child. The Erringtons' money, power and influence were widespread. And being the only child in such a family presented a challenge. Much was expected of the young lady, who was facing adolescence and impending adulthood.

It was just easier to stay to herself.

Oh . . . Marissa loved her parents very much, but she just didn't like them a whole lot. They were way too cool—as in COLD. Like ice. Sometimes she wondered if her DNA might reveal that her parents were not the two Stepford-type robots who claimed to be her mother and father. Marissa believed in God. Sadly, her parents did NOT! Marissa had always believed in Christmas, and Santa Claus and Jesus and angels. Her parents did not.

Marissa loved and adored cats, as well. Her parents, of course, did not!

Since she was little, she had dreamed of having her own little kitten. She read books about cats and even studied them on her computer. From tabbies to lions and tigers and back to tabbies, she knew all there was to know about the blessed feline. She even wrote essays and short stories about them. She prayed that one day she would have a cat of her own to love and cherish. A kitty that just might become her best friend in the whole world.

Her father made it perfectly clear that no cat would EVER live inside—or outside—of their house. Marissa disagreed, of course, and that was just one of many bones of contention she shared with her father.

Robert Errington represented the quintessential, all-American success story. An entrepreneur and computer genius, he had started his own software company just 12 years ago. *More than half the companies in the free world, as well as the United States government, now used Erringware Accounting Suite.* The Defense Department, the State Department, the C.I.A., and even the White House, depended on *Erringware.*

A few years before, Robert sold Erringware to a bigger fish for a cool ten billion dollars, while still maintaining 40% of the royalties and a seat on the board of directors. Now at age forty-five, Robert consulted to several major corporations, occupied a big seat on the board of three major banking and investment firms, and traveled the world giving speeches and such. All the while, the money came in droves. The mailman delivered dozens of checks made out to Errington every day. His wife Donna jokingly referred to the daily windfalls as "mailbox money."

It was Donna's job to gather up the checks and deposit them every week. She also gleefully took on the task of spending a good bit of the bounty as if it were so much running water. But Robert didn't seem to mind. All he cared about was "The Game." He loved to sit in front of his bank of computers and study the world's finance—to figure a way to make even more money. And he was good at it. From oil to gold, and from bonds to securities, he had the knack—the gift to know which way things were going to turn. Everything usually tilted green for Robert Errington.

Errington wasn't big on toys, but his huge Grumman executive jet was really special to him. He referred to the big, private plane as Number 3, with Numbers 2 and 1 being his family and his business. In his heart he was not really sure of the actual order of things. He would settle into one of those big, leather chairs and his staff would bring him his favorite glass of wine. The pilots would rev up those big Pratt and Whitney engines and then take off smoothly in the direction of Tokyo or London. And, in that moment, the big jet sure felt more like Number 1.

Aside from the huge mansion that he shared with his wife and only child, he did not care much about other material trappings. He did not golf or belong to country clubs or men's clubs. He did not really care about boats or even cars, although his garage was pretty full.

He left most of the socializing to Donna, and if her needs included new and bigger diamonds, fancier clothes and a new car every other month, then that was just fine with him. Robert Errington preferred to keep a lower profile and continue to play The Game! The Game was his religion. The Game was his life!

At least, that is what he thought!

* * *

It was a typical night in the Errington home. Dinner was served at six p.m., like clockwork. Tonight their longtime maid and cook, Maria, outdid herself with a mix of seafood and Mexican cuisine that was simply mouthwatering. What was also typical about the dinner was that only Marissa sat at the table. Her father was out of town, as usual, and her mom was at a charity dinner of some sort downtown.

Marissa thanked Maria for the meal and went to her room. She worked on homework for about an hour and then turned on her computer to download a new project by the Christian band, Casting Crowns, which she would then load into her iPod. She loved Casting Crowns, although the group Mercy Me was probably her favorite.

She began to search the tunes store for a possible new release by them—or maybe even Third Day—when all of a sudden the room began to spin. The girl felt dizzy and seemed right on the verge of fainting. Marissa wondered what was going on. She looked down at her hand and saw that it was trembling. Big time. Seeing her own hand shaking brought on a wave of fear.

"Oh, God, what is happening?" She began to pray. "Help me, Lord, please help me."

She tried to call out, but the scream just seemed to get caught somewhere deep inside of her throat. At that moment she realized she was going to pass out, so she desperately tried to make it to the bed. Instead, she fell flat out on the floor between her desk and her bed stand.

Marissa's room had a sliding glass door and beyond that door was a beautiful wooden deck that her dad had built for her. In the summer she would lay out on the deck in her cool and comfy chair and listen to her iPod. She was facing that very sliding door now, and just before darkness overtook her she noticed a puff of something white on the deck. The white thing seemed to have a face and the face seemed to have eyes. Shining, golden eyes that seemed to be dancing in the glare of the light that flowed out on to the deck from Marissa's lamp.

The white thing moved closer to the glass door and looked right at her. It now seemed that those gold-colored eyes were reaching right into her very soul. For some reason Marissa wasn't as frightened as she had been just the moment before.

"Oh my," she thought. *"Look at the beautiful kitty."*

Then . . . Darkness.

* * *

Maria had been cleaning up the dining room when she thought she heard something that sounded like a cat's meow. It seemed to be coming from the back door that led from the kitchen to the massive Errington garage. This was not the meow of a hungry cat. It sounded more like the call of a cat in deep distress. When Maria was a little girl growing up near Cancun, Mexico, she had several cats, and she knew their sounds. This cat was in trouble. Maria ran to the door, opened it and was nearly knocked over by a huge white ball of fur that ran right past her.

"A cat in this house will never do," she thought as she immediately gave chase to the invading creature. The cat ran through the dining room, made a hard left and then ran straight up the staircase and stopped at Marissa's bedroom door. It began to growl from deep inside its throat. The strange growl made the white cat sound almost like a dog.

As Maria topped the stairs and took a breath she could hear the growling cat. When she turned the corner and actually saw the cat she was stopped in her tracks by two things. First of all, the cat was bristled and bowed up to almost twice its normal size and, secondly, the cat had two gold-colored eyes that shined like diamonds.

"MARISSA," she yelled as she kicked open the bedroom door.

* * *

With Christmas fast approaching, Donna Errington's social schedule was just about full. It was amazing that the woman never seemed to tire of these dinners and special events and gatherings and such. She was the sole executer of the huge Errington Foundation, and every single charity organization on the planet vied for a piece of the pie. Donna relished in the self-importance of it all.

The fact was, aside from writing big checks to the worthy, and eating chicken on the charity banquet circuit, Donna didn't have much of a life at all. In younger days she and Robert had shared a whirlwind romance like no other. But as the years passed and Erringware continued to grow, the couple just slowly drifted apart.

Love and fun were like a distant memory now as each one seemed to drift around in their own time and space. Their personal agendas stood right in the middle of their marriage, and the chasm widened with each passing day. Robert was gone much of the time, and when he was home he was pre-occupied with himself and his money. Donna blocked him out for the most part and made herself content with being occupied with his money as well.

Over time their home had become a frosty windshield on a winter morning. The only warm spot was Marissa.

"What a wonderful kid," Donna thought. *"She seems to have her life together despite her surroundings."*

Donna Errington loved her daughter very much, and she still loved Robert as well. Truth be told, down deep in her heart, Donna secretly wished something extraordinary might happen that would draw them all closer to each other.

She was about to get her wish.

Her cell phone rang as another round of very mediocre food was being served. She looked down at her fancy Blackberry device and saw her own home phone number reflected on the caller ID. It was Maria. Marissa had just been rushed to a hospital.

"I am on my way!" Donna shouted.

She didn't even say goodbye to the dignitaries at her table. She ran out to the parking lot, and as she opened the driver side door of her new BMW coupe, she hit #1 and speed dialed her husband. He was 'not available at this time, so please leave a message.' She threw the Blackberry on the floor and proceeded to drive to the hospital.

* * *

Robert Errington had just landed and was on his way home. He had spent the last few days in Tokyo on behalf of Goldman Sachs. The big investment firm had asked him to take a few days to assess the information technology of their Japanese assets and ascertain what kind of upgrades they might need to implement in the coming new year. It was an easy gig for Errington, and he could have easily found the answers in a videoconference, however a plane trip to the Orient was appealing. Especially when Goldman was footing the entire bill. That thought made him smile.

He parked his Lexus in the garage and entered the home through the side door that lead to the kitchen. The house was still, as always, but there seemed to be a strange thickness in the air. A sense of dread and foreboding washed over Errington as he entered the great living room. His blood ran a bit chilly as he crossed the big room and entered his den and home office. Something wasn't right, but Errington could not put a finger on what it was. He placed his briefcase and travel bag on his desk and, as if by sheer instinct, he walked up the stairs to Marissa's room.

He knocked on her door. There was no answer. He gently pushed it open and saw that her bedside lamp was on. Marissa was not in the room. That struck him as very strange, and it only heightened the feeling that was biting and clawing at his stomach.

Suddenly, a huge white cat seemed to come out of thin air. Robert cried out, almost falling over backwards as the huge cat jumped onto Marissa's bed. The cat stared hard at him, its huge golden eyes glowing brighter and brighter.

"What is going on here? Where is Marissa and how in the world did this cat . . . "

A scared and confused Robert Errington began to fumble for his Apple phone and found that it was turned off. As the screen brightened, he saw that he had one missed call and one missed message from Donna Errington. He touched the screen in the appropriate place and heard the distant ring of his wife's Blackberry, while the big white cat continued to stare at him from Marissa's pillow.

* * *

The Erringtons, as well as their housekeeper Maria Esplante Jiminez, had been seated on leather chairs in a dreary, hospital waiting room for almost four hours now as their daughter Marissa was being operated on just one floor above them. The brain surgeon had told them that their daughter had experienced a major tear in her carotid artery, the major artery that carried blood directly to the brain.

The tear had been caused by a small aneurism that had

been lying dormant since birth. Marissa may have suffered a stroke when the tear slowed the blood flow and, right now, they were in the process of repairing the artery and would know more later on as to just how bad the damage might be.

Donna stood up, walked over to the one window in the room and stared off into space. Maria sat in a chair in the corner of the room and continued to pray. She had not stopped praying since the ambulance came for Marissa.

Robert stood up, walked over to his wife and put his arm around her shoulders. She turned to face him and then let go of her pent up emotions. The tears began to flow. She began to weep like a little girl, for perhaps the first time in many a year, as Robert took her deeper into his arms and held her tight.

Donna looked up at him and with her right hand she softly caressed his cheek. "Oh, Robert, I prayed that something might happen to draw us closer together but not this. Never this," she whispered.

"I have been a fool, Donna," answered Robert. "I have let life get away from me. I have let you and Marissa get away from me. Listen, I will take total responsibility for this and I assure you that we will do whatever it takes to save our little girl, even if I have to spend our entire . . . "

"Pardonome, Senor Robert," spoke Maria who was now standing right beside the couple. She was clutching a Bible and holding it close to her heart. "Marissa is not a piece of software and this is no business meeting. You may fire me or send me home if you wish, but I must tell you that this girl is in God's hands now, and it would do you both some good to go home now . . . and pray.

"Christmas will be here very soon and there is no Christmas tree in that house. No wreaths, no manger scenes, no angels singing praise to the Almighty Father, who now holds the life of that precious girl in His hands. That precious little saint of a daughter is the best of both of you. A little girl who loves you dearly and is not sure where SHE stands with either one of you."

"Money? Dinero?" she continued. "Money does not matter here at all. Only faith! Charity? Senora Donna, charity means LOVE in God's world, and it starts at home. I have said my piece. If I am fired now that is okay. But you two should go home and do not forget to feed that white cat. If not for her, your daughter would be in God's heaven right now, instead of upstairs. Buenos Noches, loved ones. I am praying for all of us!"

As the door closed behind Maria, Robert again turned to his wife. "She is right," he whispered. "God has given us a tremendous treasure. A wonderful daughter who is not sure where she stands with us." As he echoed Maria's words he began to cry.

"I only hope it is not too late to tell her that she means the world to us," answered Donna. "We have both been so foolish and out of touch with the things that really matter."

* * *

Marissa appeared to be on a boat of some kind. All she could see around her were clouds, although she thought she could feel small waves lapping against the hull. She really was not sure for she had never been on a boat before. She was shocked that her father didn't own a fleet of them.

The thought made her giggle for a moment. In fact, the serene and peaceful feeling that enveloped her at this very moment almost made her want to laugh out loud, and she thought that perhaps she had done just that. However the sound of her own laughter seemed distant and far away as if . . . in a dream.

Ah, that was it, she was dreaming. That was the only rational explanation for this lightness of being. She saw her mother's face as if in a mirror and her mother was crying. Then she thought she heard the voice of her father. He seemed to be praying to God and asking forgiveness. Robert Errington was actually praying?

Marissa smiled again at that one. *This has to be a dream!* The passing clouds were becoming more and more like a dense fog that seemed to envelope her, yet she could still make out a bright light in the distance. Anyhow, that is what it seemed like. She tried to sit up. Had she been lying down? There was something laying beside her and pressing its weight against her side. She quickly came to the realization that it was a cat. It was the white cat with the golden eyes.

The kitty rose up on all fours and stared at Marissa. Her feline eyes were all aglow. The cat meowed once and then settled into a smooth and relaxing purr. She continued to stare at Marissa. The clouds began to fade and the light seemed all the brighter. The cat purred even louder.

"Oh, how sweet," whispered Marissa. "You are still with me."

"Sweet Mother of our Savior, she is waking up!"

"Maria," thought Marissa. *"Was that Maria?"*

The bright light began to turn into the huge Italian made lamp in the living room of her home. Marissa opened her eyes and saw her mother and father looking at her. They were weeping and holding onto each other very tightly. She could still hear Maria's voice somewhere in the distance. She seemed to be singing a Gospel song.

"What is going on?" Marissa asked. Her throat felt dry and a bit hoarse.

"God has blessed us, honey. That is what is going on,"

said Donna Errington through a cloud of tears.

"He has given us back our little girl," added Robert. 'We are so very grateful."

Donna explained what had happened. She told Marissa about the aneurism and the operations and the possible stroke and brain damage. She told her daughter how they had brought her home and how she had been sleeping for a long time. Robert added that the doctor was on his way but was very encouraged by what was going on. It would seem that Marissa Errington would be just fine.

"What day is this, Mom?" asked Marissa.

"It is Christmas, honey. Look around."

There was a big tree decorated with bright lights in one corner of the room and a ton of presents underneath. There were wreaths and angels and a beautiful manger scene. The house looked and felt and smelled like Christmas itself.

It had never been this way before. Not EVER

"Things will be different around here from now on," said her father, as he held her hand. "I sold the jet. My only job now is a consultant for *Erringware*. No more trips unless we go as a family. Your mother will be home a lot more, as well. She will still make foundation decisions but mostly from her office upstairs. You, my sweet daughter, will also take a leadership role in the foundation. I want to pay God back for His blessings, and I want and NEED your help in that effort."

"What a Christmas," thought Marissa. "What a miracle! Thank you, Jesus. Oh, THANK YOU."

With all that was going on, Marissa had not thought about the kitty. As if on cue, the cat stretched and meowed quite loudly. This was another miracle for certain. There was actually a cat in the house.

The big, white cat came close to Marissa's face and looked right into her eyes. The golden-colored eyes seemed to glow just as they had from the moment she first saw this very special kitty on her deck. Marissa petted the cat and playfully asked, "Just what part have YOU played in all of this?"

"That cat saved your life, Marissa," said Robert with a smile. "Maria says she is an angel cat and named her Snowball!"

"Snowball, huh?" said Marissa as the cat continued to purr. "Well, that is a perfect name."

She picked up the beautiful, white kitty and held her close to her cheek.

"I love you, Snowball. It seems that both us have found a new home."

MERRY CHRISTMAS. (JSB)

Authors note: This story is dedicated to the memory of our Lily White. She was a good kitty!

Little Jerry's Christmas ~ The Play

As a bonus, we are including a dramatic version of Little Jerry's Christmas for use by your church, school, or drama group.
BLESSINGS (JSB)

THREE SCENES, Two Sets

Living Room for Scene #1 (being decorated), Tavern Set for Scene #2 (bar, stools, etc.), and Living Room for Scene #3 (fully decorated, Little Jerry's bedroom to the side, optional)

Characters:
Little Jerry 10 or 11 years old
Mom mid- to late thirties
Big Jerry mid- to late thirties
Marty The Bartender
Man In White

SCENE ONE: (A big city type row house living room, a couch, some chairs, a TV, etc. and a Christmas tree standing in one corner of the room. We find Little Jerry and his mom decorating the tree, with boxes of decorations all around mom, who is humming a Christmas song. Little Jerry seems just miserable.)

Mom: "Why so glum, kiddo? I thought Christmastime was your favorite time of the year."

LJ: "It is. I guess. It is just that . . . oh well . . ."

Mom: "I know, honey, you are mad at Daddy again—and well, so am I. He should be here with us instead of out there . . . (Her voice trails off a bit.) But you must admit this happens to be one fine and beautiful tree. I appreciate your helping me drag it home from Haggerty's used car lot."

LJ: "It is a good thing he sells trees at Christmas, because he sure never sells any cars. Those same cars and trucks are there every year."

Mom: "Well, I know the Haggerty's, and they sure don't have much. But around this neighborhood . . . who does?"

LJ: "He should sell Corvettes or Cadillacs or something!"

Mom: "Right . . . and when have you ever seem cars like that around here?"

(They both laugh out loud, but then LJ looks sad again.)

LJ: "If Daddy would quit drinking and losing his job every other month, maybe WE could be riding around in a nicer car. Sometimes I just hate him, Mom!"

(Mom kneels down and hugs her son tightly as he begins to weep. She guides him over to the couch, and they sit very close to each other. She gently takes both of Little Jerry's hands into hers and begins to speak softly and lovingly to her son.)

Mom: "Now listen to me . . . your father loves us both very much. He is going through a tough time right now. But listen, he IS a good man. He fought in the war and all of that has changed him somehow."

LJ: "I know all of that, Mom. I don't really hate Daddy, but sometimes I just do not like him very much. It is hard to find the GOOD man when I am always wondering which drunk is coming home on some nights. The funny drunk or the mean drunk or even the sad, army guy drunk. I just want Daddy to come home. It's Christmas, Mom . . . where is he?"

(Mom looks reflective.)

Mom: "The funny drunk reminds me of your dad before the war, always smiling and laughing and cracking jokes. The mean drunk scares me to death, and the 'sad army guy drunk,' as you put it, is indeed the saddest of all. He has been through so very much, Jerry. I DO wish I knew where he was tonight!"

LJ: "Do you want me to get my bike and check out all the taprooms in the neighborhood like I usually do?"

Mom: (smiling) "Not tonight, son. Not tonight."

LJ: "Where is the manger scene, Mom?"

Mom: It is in that red box. Go ahead and unpack it. Christmas is not Christmas without it, you know!"

LJ: "I love how the little white light bulb lights up the Baby Jesus.

(As little Jerry unpacks the manger scene, Mom walks back over by the tree and reaches down into another box. She brings forth the most beautiful, white angel figurine. Jerry smiles when he sees it.)

LJ: "Cool, Mom . . . The ANGEL!"

Mom: "I have had this Angel since I was your age, Jerry."

(She climbs up on a step stool and gently places the Angel on top of the tree. She and Jerry stare at it for a while in silence.)

LJ: "Maybe this year God will heal Daddy and send him home to us."

Mom: "Let's ask Him to do just that, honey."

(Mom and LJ get down on their knees in front of the tree. Mom reaches for LJ's hand and holds onto it tightly as she begins to pray softly.)

Mom: "Dear Precious and Heavenly Father, I ask you tonight to look after my husband. He IS a good man, and he has suffered greatly and been through so much. I pray tonight,

Heavenly Father, that on this Christmas Eve you might see fit to bless him and forgive him and love him. And if it be Thy will, bring him home to this house—and to me and to his son, who DO love him so very much. We need him here, oh Lord, and he needs YOU . . . in his heart and in his life. You are the Master of all, and You have said in Your Word that You would lift our heavy burdens. Well, Lord, I just cannot take much more. Please, God, make him stop drinking. Help him to live with the deaths of those other soldiers and be the husband and father he should be. God, I know You are able to do this and—on this night when many years ago You saw fit to give us Your only, precious Son—I thought perhaps You might have mercy on a mother and HER son, who really need a blessing. Thank You . . . in Jesus name. Amen."

(LJ stands up and stares at the white Angel atop the tree and begins to speak to it in a prayerful, childlike way.)

LJ: "Mister Angel, I know there are angels for real. My mom taught me that they are everywhere and that each of us has a special one just to watch over us kids. So, if it is not too much trouble, could you please speak to God and ask Him to answer my mom's prayers tonight? Please bring my father home, *ummmm* sober, if that's okay. Also, please tell God I love Him, too, and I thank Him for Baby Jesus. Amen."

Mom: "Let's go to bed now, son, Merry Christmas."

LJ: "Merry Christmas, Mom."

(Mom exits stage left and Jerry walks into the other room and crawls into his bed and pulls the covers up to his chin.)

LJ: "Goodnight, Daddy. I love you!" (Lights dim.)

END OF SCENE

SCENE TWO: (A neighborhood tavern. Three characters, BIG JERRY sitting at the bar, Marty the bartender and a tall, classy man in a white suit. Scene opens with just Big Jerry sitting at the bar and Marty behind the bar.)

Big Jerry: "How about another round, Marty. A Boilermaker this time. A tall draft and a healthy shot of good bourbon whiskey should do the trick."

Marty: "You have already had four, Jerry."

BJ: "Well, it usually takes five, Marty . . . or six." (Big Jerry's voice trails off a bit.)

Marty: "Takes five or six to do just what, man?"

BJ: "It takes that many to keep me from seeing myself in that desert."

Marty: "Listen, friend. It's Christmas Eve. You are the only one in here tonight. Just drink up and go home so I can close this place and go home myself."

(Big Jerry slugs down the drink and places the glass down hard on the bar.)

BJ: "Another round, Marty! NOW!" (His voice begins to slur badly.)

(Marty leans over the bar and speaks softly.)

Marty: "This is the last one buddy . . . and I mean it. You have a family at home."

BJ: "Well, dead soldiers have families too you know . . ."

(Big Jerry begins to weep, his voice slurring badly.)

Marty: "What is up with you, man?"

BJ: It's a deep, dark hole, Marty, and I just cannot climb out of it. I can't handle it anymore. I see them laughing and then all of a sudden they are gone . . . GONE . . . and all because of me. I feel so guilty all the time . . . I NEED FORGIVNESS MARTY . . . FORGIVNESS"

(Big Jerry leans forward and rests his head on the edge of the bar as Marty walks to the other side of the room and begins to clean up the place.
Man in white suit enters bar. He softly shuts the door behind him, saunters over to the bar and takes a seat beside Big Jerry. He speaks in a proper tone, almost as an Englishman might speak.)

Man In White: "Forgiveness, Jerry? Forgiveness for just what, I might ask."

BJ: (Raises his head and looks right into the man's eyes. His speech is more slurred than ever.) "Forgiveness for just being alive!"

MIW: "Life is a great gift, Jerry. It is not your fault Sergeant Briscoe and Private First Class Benton are not here today. That was NOT your decision to make, you know."

BJ: "But I could have . . ."

MIW: "Could have WHAT, Jerry? You were a few yards away getting ammo when the mortar hit. It is all as simple as that! The world revolves. Things happen . . . we turn left or we turn right. We go up. We go down. We live . . . we die. There was nothing you could have done that day. The war was hard enough with all the killing and death everywhere. No reason to keep blaming yourself for something you had no control over."

BJ: "But . . . Sir . . . I . . ."

MIW: "Get in the ballgame, soldier. You have a precious wife and son at home right now who love you . . . and need you. Besides, it is CHRISTMAS. Sober up, man . . . and that is an order."

(Jerry begins to tremble and then weep uncontrollably. Then he pulls himself together a bit and again looks at the man in white.)

BJ: "Who ARE you, sir?"

MIW: "I am just another soldier as well, Jerry, and by the authority of HE, Who sent me to this wretched and foul smelling place . . . HE, Who holds the universe in the palm of His hand . . . HE, Who holds the keys of life and death . . . HE, Who was born of a virgin on this very day, two thousand years ago and died on a cross for YOU, Jerry. By HIS authority I plead with you to get your act together and go home to your family . . . to seek the will of Jesus Christ in your life and to quit all of this drinking and feeling sorry for yourself. Be the man HE wants you to be. It IS possible to do this, Jerry, I assure you. Have faith in Him. Accept CHRIST into your heart and life as your Savior and go home! Go before you lose it all . . . Merry Christmas, Jerry."

(The man in white exits, walking right by Marty, who continues to wipe tables and such. Big Jerry again places his head down on the bar and in a few moments he stops crying. He looks up and quickly realizes the man in white is gone. He yells out to Marty.)

BJ: "Hey, Marty. Did you get the name of that guy in the fancy white suit?"

Marty: "What man? Only you and me in this place tonight, and we are both about to be gone because, like I said before (Marty's voice gets louder and louder), I am closing 'er up and going to the house. In other words, last call, partner!"

BJ: "Never mind. How much do I owe you?"

Marty: (voice back to normal) "You don't owe me a thing, soldier. Just go on home! Get outtahere!"

(Big Jerry grabs his coat and heads for the door. His speaking voice is no longer slurred. He turns to Marty, a big smile on his face.)

BJ: "That is just what I am going to do, Marty, old boy, I am heading for the house. But first I need to make a few stops. I think several stores are still open this late.

(BJ is putting on his coat as he speaks.)

Marty: "Hey, yo, big guy, how did you sober up so quick? A minute ago you were comatose, man!"

BJ: "It is God, Marty. It is the saving and forgiving power of his Son Jesus Christ. It is what Christmas is all about. See ya around."

(Big Jerry leaves quickly and the door slams behind him.)

Marty: "Yeah, see ya around Jerry. Merry Christmas . . ."
 (Marty speaks to the now empty room, while wiping the bar with a rag. Go dark.)

END OF SCENE

SCENE THREE: (Living Room scene. The Angel shines brightly atop the lighted tree and presents of all kinds are under the tree. The manger scene is almost put together, and the little light bulb inside of it shines brightly. We can hear *Silent Night* playing in the background. We find Big Jerry and his wife sitting on the couch murmuring softly and lovingly to each other as the lights come up. Little Jerry is in his bed sleeping.)

Mom: "You have told me this so many times before, Jerry. Then you always backslide into that dark place, and it is so hard on Little Jerry and me. I so WANT to believe you. I NEED to believe you.

BJ: "Honey, I know what I have put you through, but this time it is real. God has shown me I need to get beyond the horrors of battle and 'man up' a bit. To be the kind of husband and father He wants me to be. I will never forget those men, but somehow I feel different about it all now. I want . . . I want my family to come first now. I can and WILL do this!"

Mom: "The things you saw and did over there were very meaningful, dear husband. You heard the call and answered that call for all of us. I am proud of you for your service to America. I always will be, as will be your son. But right now the war is over for you. Little Jerry needs a father and . . . I need a husband."

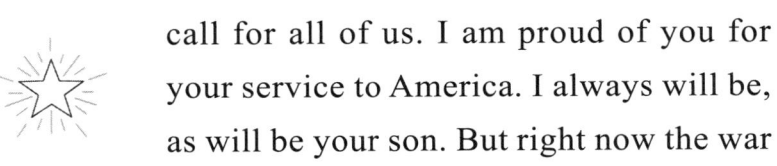

BJ: "I love you, hon. I always have."

Mom: "I love you too, with all of my heart."

(BJ takes his wife into his arms and holds on to her. Somewhere during the conversation between BJ and Mom, LJ wakes up and begins to listen. He softly gets out of bed and walks to the side of the living room, sleepy eyed and in his pajamas. If there is no bedroom, he can just appear there from the side of the stage.

After Mom's last line Little Jerry begins to slowly enter the room. BJ and Mom stand up, and they all just look at each other for a moment, then Big Jerry kneels down on one knee and spreads his arms wide open. Little Jerry runs into his arms, and the man holds his son to his breast as mom begins to weep tears of joy.)

LJ: "You are home! You are HOME! Didja mean what ya said, Dad?"

BJ: "Every word, son. Every word! I am home now . . . God has forgiven me, and so has your mother."

(LJ looks up at his mom who is fighting back tears of joy.)

LJ: "We are going to be okay then, right Mom?

Mom: "We are going to be just fine, son. Merry Christmas!"

THE END

☆

The Bell . . . Christmas Commentary

A final thought from your author. (JSB)

In the wonderful movie The Polar Express, based on the award winning children's book written by Chris Van Allsberg, a bell from Santa's sleigh is the centerpiece of the story. As the young boy gets older and more doubtful of Santa Claus, he finds he can no longer hear the sleigh bells on Santa's sleigh. Eventually, after a dream ride on a magical train to the North Pole, he overcomes his skepticism and Santa gives him a bell as a Christmas gift—a bell he can hear as long as he believes in the magic of Christmas!

As I left the theater with my wife and grandkids in tow, I thought about the New Jersey State Legislature wanting to ban all Christmas music in schools, including music that has anything to do with Santa Claus.

Yes, you read that right. Not Jesus . . . Santa Claus. Under the influence of our old friends the American Civil Liberties Union (ACLU), this crazy legislation is actually being considered, and most feel IT WILL PASS!

I guess in their loony, political way of thinking, when kids think of Santa, they will think of Christmas, and perhaps then . . . think of the real meaning of Christmas, which IS the birth of Jesus.

Of course, we certainly can NOT have that!

Now, songs about snow and winter are okay. *Winter Wonderland* is in. *Here Comes Santa Claus* is out. *Frosty The Snowman* walks a fine line, but he makes the cut. However, Rudolph . . . OUTTAHERE! By the way, I am not even talking about LYRICS . . . canned, pumped in Muzak versions of Christmas songs like those we hear in the shopping mall and on elevators, can NOT be played in the schools, bucko. I suppose thoughts of what Christmas is all about just may scar children for life!

I would imagine, if they could, the legislative wackos would ban *The Polar Express* movie, as well as the book. There may even be a moratorium placed on *It's A Wonderful Life* (there IS an angel in it, you know) and *Miracle on 34th Street* (Santa again, disguised as Kris Kringle!). *Sound out*landish and farfetched? Well, in my mind it already is—all of that and then some.

Parents should be carrying torches and pitchforks. What in the name of all that is right is wrong with kids believing in Santa Claus . . . or the Easter Bunny and Tooth Fairy, for that matter? It is called . . . are you ready? I-M-A-G-I-N-A-T-I-O-N! Dangerous? Yes! I'll tell you why. Some adults actually grow up with these childhood thoughts and memories still intact. Some adults do not kill off the child that dwells inside their being.

You know, that little boy or little girl who still exists in your heart? You can see that child in the sparkle of one's eyes. Heaven help the man or woman who does not still have that spark because that would mean the child inside is gone. And they will never again hear the bell.

When I was little I used to sleep in my bedroom and dream about Santa. I also used to dream about one day singing in a great quartet and traveling in a big bus all around the country. I believed in Santa Claus, and I guarantee you that little Joey could hear the magical reindeer bringing the sleigh full of toys as it zipped across the sky in North Philly.   I still hear him, so I guess I am loony as well. New Jersey may ban ME from the state (which would be awful because my sister Nancy still lives there).

My parents made sure that Christmas Morning was like Disneyland for my sister and me, even though money was not in abundant supply on Jasper Street. Many of my fondest memories center around Christmas . . . Christmas songs, Christmas Eve and Christmas Day are all still very magical to me, and I am sixty years old. I still cry over the cane left by the fireplace. I still get weepy over Zu Zu's petals. I still get emotional over Prancer turning out to be the real deal at the end of the story. I cry inside for those children who do not know what Christmas is all about, and I cry more for the adults who stifle this wondrous spirit.

Little Joey is still alive—and Virginia, there IS a Santa Claus. There was a virgin birth, as well, and a Savior born who one day died on a cross for our sins. It is not all about money and presents and credit cards and what IS and what is NOT politically correct. It is about letting a little magic into your life and keeping the child inside your heart alive and vibrant.

When that spark flickers and dies . . . when we let go of childhood totally . . . start packing, because we are nearing the end of the trail!

So keep listening and keep believing.

Can you hear the bell?

MERRY CHRISTMAS (JSB)

Authors note: This little commentary was inspired by the New Jersey Legislature, the ACLU, The Polar Express and my wife Mary Ann, who just yesterday morning turned to me with misty eyes and proclaimed, "I think that in my heart . . . I am STILL little Mary!"

Yes! Indeed she is!

The Carpenter's Choice... An Epilogue
by Joseph S. Bonsall

He was a good man . . . a righteous man And very much in love. She was the girl of his dreams and all he thought about. With his own hands he would build her a home and provide for her a happy life. He would be kind and he would be true. A man of conviction . . . he knew what a man was supposed to do.

To work hard . . . provide . . . be faithful and true. Let God lead.
He was good with a hammer and wood so he would build . . . a future.

What would you have done in Joseph's place?

He knew what his religion required but he was still reluctant to cast his wife aside. She could be persecuted and even stoned if this word got out. What's a righteous man NOW to do?

Obviously, Joseph did the right thing. He stood by his young wife as she gave birth to the Lamb of God and then went on to protect her and love her as a husband should.

I have always been fascinated with the story of Joseph, although there is not a whole lot about him in the Bible. Once he hurries Mary and Jesus out of town after the angelic warning, he very quickly takes a backseat, first to his blessed wife Mary; and then he is quickly overshadowed by the greatest story ever told. The Savior of the world . . . born of a virgin . . . to die on a cross and rise up in triumph therefore conquering the grave and sin itself, in order to provide a pathway to everlasting life for those of us who believe in HIM. A pathway paid for in Sacrifice . . . and Blood!

Jesus Christ, who was NOT the son of the carpenter, but the Son of God in Heaven.

But, oh that night . . . when his young and very beautiful bride told him that she was with child and yet no man had touched her. What a pill that must have been to swallow, and yet the Bible tells us that Joseph indeed considered the miracle even before the Angel appeared unto him to confirm the truth of it all. Joseph took up the mantle of responsibility that came with being the surrogate. I am certain that after the confusion Joseph was willing and able to do all that he could do to help raise this mighty Miracle.

Again . . . we learn very little of those twelve years before Jesus spoke at the temple, but it is easy to picture Joseph being the good father and mentor to the young boy. God must have been so proud of the way this was all handled by a simple carpenter, and I am certain that a wonderful place was prepared in Glory for this righteous man.

The Oak Ridge Boys have a wonderful new song on our new *Christmas Time's A-Coming* project called *Getting Ready For A Baby* that sweetly tells the story of Joseph and Mary preparing for birth, much like any other couple and yet . . . so much more extraordinary. It is a great song that brings the human element into play, and it is that human element that interests your author and has inspired this little epilogue.

The lesson here is simple. At Christmastime or ANY time when it seems like the load is getting too hard to bear, or when your personal life is in shambles, or when big decisions have to be examined or sickness or even death looms, it is important to know that even in this fast-paced day and age God HAS a PLAN.

There will always be choices to make. Which fork does one take? Our human emotions alone wreak fear and havoc on one's being and, like Joseph, we must make a stand.

The best and most important choice we can make is deciding to trust in HIM with all of our heart and lean upon the

Everlasting Arms of Jesus Christ in ALL things!

THIS was the Carpenter's Choice, and it is my prayer that those of you who have taken the time to read my little stories about miracles at Christmastime will also come to love and follow the GREATEST Miracle of all.

Like the Angel told Emily and Eric, "For unto YOU is BORN . . Serve The Master!"

Let us SERVE the MASTER . . . on Christmas Day . . . and EVERY day!